The Phoenix King

Fairy tales, Folk tales, Legends & Mythology, Volume 3

Patrick William Lee

Published by Starlit Tales Publishing, 2024.

This is a work of fiction. Similarities to real people, places, or events are entirely coincidental.

THE PHOENIX KING

First edition. August 20, 2024.

Copyright © 2024 Patrick William Lee.

ISBN: 979-8227587428

Written by Patrick William Lee.

Table of Contents

To those who believe in the power of renewal and the strength found in the balance of life and death. To the dreamers who see beyond the flames, the seekers who embrace both light and darkness, and to all who strive to restore harmony in their own worlds. May the legend of the Phoenix King ignite your spirit and remind you that even in the ashes, there is hope for rebirth. This tale is for you.

Chapter 1: Introduction: The Legend of the Phoenix King

Prologue: The World of Eldoria

In the ancient world of Eldoria, where magic and mystery intertwined with the fabric of reality, the skies shimmered with hues of lavender and gold, and the land was vibrant with life both wondrous and terrifying. Eldoria was a world where the elements were not mere forces of nature but living, breathing entities. Rivers sang as they flowed, the winds whispered secrets, and the earth rumbled with the pulse of an ancient heartbeat. But among these forces, it was fire that held the most revered place, for fire was the essence of life and death, the beginning and the end.

Eldoria was a vast realm, divided into several kingdoms, each governed by the elemental forces. There was the Kingdom of Aqualis, ruled by the merfolk who could command the oceans and summon storms with a wave of their hands. The Kingdom of Sylva, where the treefolk dwelled, guardians of the ancient forests and custodians of the earth's secrets. The Kingdom of Zephyra, where the air spirits danced on the wind, their ethereal forms ever-changing as they moved with the breeze. And then, there was the Phoenix Kingdom, the land of fire, where the flames were eternal, and the air was thick with the scent of embers.

The Phoenix Kingdom, or Ignis, as it was known in the ancient tongue, was a land of contrasts. Its terrain was harsh, with towering volcanoes that spewed molten lava, and vast deserts where the sands glowed under the scorching sun. Yet, amid this unforgiving landscape, there was beauty—crimson flowers that bloomed in the heat, their petals like tongues of fire, and crystal lakes of lava that shimmered under the night sky. The people of Ignis, known as the Fireborn, were as resilient as their land, their spirits unyielding, and their hearts ablaze with passion.

At the heart of Ignis lay the Sacred Flame, a massive fire that burned with an otherworldly intensity. It was said that the Sacred Flame was the source of all fire in Eldoria, a gift from the gods themselves. The Fireborn revered the Sacred Flame, for it was the very essence of their existence, the source of their power and their connection to the elemental forces. But more than that, the Sacred Flame was the cradle of their kings—the Phoenix Kings, who were born from the fire and destined to rule.

The Phoenix Kings were not ordinary rulers. They were beings of immense power, born from the Sacred Flame, with the ability to control fire and rise from their own ashes. They were immortal, their reigns lasting centuries, and they were tasked with maintaining the balance between life and death, creation and destruction. For fire, in Eldoria, was not merely a tool of war or warmth—it was the force that kept the world in harmony.

The Prophecy of the Phoenix King

Long ago, before the time of the Fireborn, before even the first Phoenix King, there was a prophecy. It was whispered by the winds, inscribed in the ancient stones, and guarded by the oldest of the fire spirits. The prophecy spoke of a time of great turmoil when the balance of Eldoria would be shattered, and darkness would threaten to consume the land. It was a time when the elemental forces would be thrown into chaos, and the world would be on the brink of destruction.

In this time of need, the prophecy foretold, a Phoenix King would rise—a king unlike any before, born from the purest flame, with the power to bring balance to the world. This Phoenix King would be the embodiment of the Eternal Flame, a being of light and fire, destined to restore harmony between the elements and renew the cycle of life and death. But this king's journey would not be easy, for the forces of darkness would rise against him, seeking to extinguish his flame and plunge Eldoria into eternal night.

The prophecy was both a blessing and a curse, a beacon of hope and a warning of the trials to come. The Fireborn lived by it, their lives shaped by its words, their hopes pinned on the arrival of the prophesied Phoenix King. For centuries, they waited, each Phoenix King that rose from the Sacred Flame hailed as the potential savior, but none fulfilled the prophecy. The flames burned bright, the kings ruled with strength and wisdom, but the true Phoenix King, the one foretold by the prophecy, had yet to emerge.

The Birth of the Phoenix King

The time of the prophecy drew near, and the Sacred Flame burned with an intensity that had not been seen in millennia. The Fireborn knew that the time had come, that the Phoenix King of prophecy was about to be born. The night was still, the air heavy with anticipation, as the Fireborn gathered around the Sacred Flame, their eyes fixed on the fire that had given birth to their kings for generations.

The flames roared, growing higher and higher, until they reached the sky. The ground trembled, and the air crackled with energy as the fire took shape. It was a magnificent sight—an inferno of reds, oranges, and golds, swirling and dancing in a display of raw power. And from the heart of this inferno, a figure began to emerge.

At first, it was just a silhouette, a shadow within the flames. But as the figure stepped forward, it became clear that this was no ordinary being. The flames seemed to cling to the figure, wrapping around it like a cloak, and as it emerged fully from the fire, the Fireborn gasped in awe. Before them stood a phoenix, unlike any they had ever seen.

This phoenix was enormous, its wingspan stretching across the sky, its feathers glowing with a radiant light. Its eyes were like twin suns, burning with an intensity that seemed to pierce through the very soul. As it spread its wings, the air shimmered with heat, and the Fireborn could feel the power emanating from the creature—a power that was both terrifying and awe-inspiring.

This was no ordinary phoenix. This was the Phoenix King, the one foretold by the prophecy. Born from the purest flame, with the power to bring balance to the world. As the phoenix stood before the Sacred Flame, it let out a cry—a sound that echoed through the land, a call that resonated with the very essence of Eldoria.

The Fireborn fell to their knees, their hearts filled with reverence and hope. They knew that this was the moment they had been waiting for, the moment the prophecy had foretold. The Phoenix King had arrived, and with him came the promise of a new era—a time of balance, renewal, and hope.

But the Phoenix King's journey was just beginning. The prophecy had spoken of great trials, of battles to be fought, and sacrifices to be made. The Phoenix King would need to harness the power of the Eternal Flame, face the forces of darkness, and restore the balance between life and death. It would be a journey of fire and ash, of destruction and renewal, of light and darkness.

And so, the legend of the Phoenix King began—a tale of a king born from fire, destined to rise from the ashes and bring balance to a world on the brink of destruction. It was a story that would be told for generations, a story of hope and sacrifice, of power and wisdom. The world of Eldoria would never be the same, for the Phoenix King had risen, and with him came the promise of a brighter future.

The World Awaits

As the legend of the Phoenix King spread across Eldoria, the world held its breath. The other kingdoms—Aqualis, Sylva, Zephyra—each reacted in their own way. The merfolk of Aqualis watched the skies, their minds troubled by the tales of fire and prophecy. The treefolk of Sylva whispered among the ancient oaks, their roots sensing the shifting balance of the world. The air spirits of Zephyra danced on the wind, their laughter tinged with a note of unease.

But it was not only the elemental kingdoms that felt the change. In the shadows of Eldoria, forces long forgotten stirred, awakened by the birth of the Phoenix King. Dark entities, ancient and powerful, sensed the rising power of the flame and began to move. They knew that the time of the prophecy had come, and with it, the chance to seize control of the world.

Among these dark forces was the Volcano God, an ancient deity of fire and destruction, who had long harbored a grudge against the Phoenix Kings. The Volcano God believed that fire was a force of pure destruction, meant to cleanse the world of its impurities. The idea of balance, of fire as a force of both creation and renewal, was an affront to his very nature. And so, when he learned of the birth of the prophesied Phoenix King, he saw it as a direct challenge to his power—a challenge he would not ignore.

The Volcano God was not the only one who felt threatened. In the farthest reaches of Eldoria, in the cold, dark corners of the world where light had long been extinguished, a dark phoenix stirred. Born from the ashes of hatred and despair, this dark phoenix was the embodiment of destruction, a creature of pure malevolence. It had waited for centuries, biding its time, gathering strength in the shadows. And now, with the birth of the Phoenix King, it saw its opportunity to rise.

The Phoenix King's journey would not be easy. The forces arrayed against him were formidable, and the challenges he would face would test not only his strength but his very soul. He would need to master the power of the Eternal Flame, confront the darkness within himself, and make sacrifices that would shape the future of Eldoria.

But the Phoenix King was not alone. The Fireborn, his people, stood ready to support him. The ancient fire spirits watched over him, offering their guidance and wisdom. And in the heart of the Phoenix Kingdom, the Sacred Flame burned ever brighter, a symbol of hope and resilience.

The world of Eldoria was at a crossroads, poised between light and darkness, creation and destruction. The birth of the Phoenix King marked the beginning of a new era—an era that would be defined by his choices, his battles, and his sacrifices. The legend of the Phoenix King had begun, and with it, the story of a world on the brink of transformation.

The Legacy of the Flame

As the Phoenix King prepared for the journey ahead, the Fireborn gathered around the Sacred Flame, their hearts filled with a mixture of hope and trepidation. They knew that the road before their king would be fraught with danger, that the trials he would face would be unlike any before. But they also knew that the Phoenix King was their only hope—the one who could restore balance to Eldoria and ensure the survival of their world.

The elders of the Phoenix Kingdom, the Keepers of the Flame, convened in a council to discuss the prophecy and the role their king would play in the times to come. These elders were wise and ancient, their knowledge passed down through generations. They had seen many Phoenix Kings rise and fall, and they understood the weight of the prophecy that hung over their land.

"The prophecy speaks of balance," one of the elders said, his voice grave. "Balance between life and death, creation and destruction. But balance is not easily achieved. It requires sacrifice, wisdom, and the strength to make difficult choices."

Another elder, her face lined with the marks of time, nodded in agreement. "The Phoenix King must be prepared for the trials ahead. He will face forces that seek to upset the balance, forces that will stop at nothing to see him fail. But he must not waver. He must hold fast to the principles of the Eternal Flame, for only then can he bring about the renewal that Eldoria so desperately needs."

The council continued their deliberations, their voices echoing through the chamber. They spoke of the challenges the Phoenix King would face—the dark phoenix that sought to consume him, the Volcano God who wished to destroy him, and the internal struggles that would test his resolve. They knew that the Phoenix King's journey would be a difficult one, but they also knew that he was the one foretold by the prophecy, the one who could bring about the balance that Eldoria had long awaited.

As the council came to a close, the elders turned their attention to the Sacred Flame, their hearts heavy with the weight of their decisions. They knew that they could not protect the Phoenix King from the trials ahead, but they could offer him their guidance and support. And so, with solemn hearts, they pledged their loyalty to their king, vowing to stand by his side as he embarked on his journey.

The Path Forward

With the prophecy echoing in his mind, the Phoenix King stood before the Sacred Flame, his eyes reflecting the fiery light. He could feel the weight of his destiny, the expectations of his people, and the challenges that lay ahead. But he also felt a sense of purpose, a burning desire to fulfill the prophecy and bring balance to his world.

The Phoenix King knew that his journey would not be easy, that he would face enemies both old and new, and that he would need to master the power of the Eternal Flame. But he also knew that he was not alone. The Fireborn stood ready to support him, the elders offered their wisdom, and the Sacred Flame burned ever bright, a constant reminder of the power and responsibility he carried.

As the Phoenix King prepared to set out on his journey, he took one last look at the Sacred Flame, feeling its warmth and energy flow through him. This was the beginning of his story, the start of a legend that would be told for generations to come. He was the Phoenix King, the one born from fire, the one destined to rise from the ashes and bring balance to a world on the brink of destruction.

And with that, the Phoenix King spread his wings, the flames igniting around him, and took to the skies. His journey had begun, and with it, the legend of the Phoenix King—a tale of fire and ash, of hope and sacrifice, of light and darkness, and of a king who would rise to bring balance to Eldoria.

The world watched as the Phoenix King soared into the night, his fiery form lighting up the sky. The prophecy had been set in motion, the forces of darkness were stirring, and the balance of Eldoria hung in the balance. But the Phoenix King was ready, and with the power of the Eternal Flame, he would face whatever challenges lay ahead.

The legend of the Phoenix King had begun, and the world of Eldoria would never be the same again.

Chapter 1: Birth in the Flames

The Phoenix Kingdom: Realm of Eternal Fire

In the vast world of Eldoria, where the elemental forces of nature reigned supreme, the Phoenix Kingdom, or Ignis as it was known in the ancient tongue, was a land unlike any other. It was a realm where fire was not merely a tool or a destructive force—it was the very essence of life and death, the beginning and the end. The Phoenix Kingdom was a place where the flames never ceased to burn, where the air was thick with the scent of embers, and where the people lived in harmony with the fire that surrounded them.

The kingdom was nestled within a range of towering volcanoes, their peaks often obscured by plumes of smoke and ash. Rivers of molten lava flowed through the valleys, their glowing paths illuminating the darkened skies. The ground beneath was a mosaic of obsidian and igneous rock, a testament to the land's fiery origins. Yet, despite the harshness of the environment, the Phoenix Kingdom was a place of incredible beauty. Crimson flowers, known as Emberblooms, dotted the landscape, their petals glowing with an inner light. Crystal-clear lakes of lava shimmered under the starlit sky, their surfaces reflecting the brilliant hues of the flames.

The people of the Phoenix Kingdom, known as the Fireborn, were as resilient and enduring as the land they inhabited. They were a proud and noble race, with skin that bore the marks of their fiery heritage—often tinged with shades of bronze, copper, or gold. Their eyes glowed with the inner fire that connected them to the Sacred Flame, the source of all life in the kingdom. The Fireborn were fierce warriors, skilled in the art of battle, but they were also wise and deeply spiritual, understanding the delicate balance between creation and destruction.

At the heart of the Phoenix Kingdom lay the Sacred Flame, a colossal fire that burned with an intensity beyond mortal comprehension. It was said that the Sacred Flame was a gift from the gods, a manifestation of the Eternal Flame that existed at the center of all creation. The Sacred Flame was the source of the Fireborn's power, their connection to the elemental forces of fire. It was also the cradle of their kings—the Phoenix Kings, who were born from the flame and destined to rule.

The Phoenix Kings were more than just rulers; they were the embodiment of the kingdom's spirit, beings of immense power who could control fire and rise from their own ashes. They were immortal, their reigns lasting centuries, and they were tasked with maintaining the balance between life and death, creation and destruction. For in the Phoenix Kingdom, fire was not just a symbol—it was the force that kept the world in harmony, ensuring that life continued in its eternal cycle.

The Birth of the Phoenix King

The time had come, as foretold by the prophecy, for the birth of a Phoenix King who would change the course of history. The prophecy had been whispered through the ages, passed down from generation to generation, and it spoke of a king born from the purest flame, one who would rise to bring balance to the world of Eldoria. The Fireborn had awaited this moment for centuries, their hopes and dreams pinned on the arrival of the prophesied king.

On the night of the prophesied birth, the Phoenix Kingdom was still, the usual roar of the flames reduced to a hushed whisper as if the very land itself held its breath in anticipation. The skies above Ignis were a deep, dark red, the stars hidden behind a veil of smoke and ash. The Sacred Flame burned brighter than ever, its flames reaching towards the heavens, casting a warm, golden glow over the gathered Fireborn.

The Fireborn, led by the High Priests of the Flame, assembled around the Sacred Flame, their faces lit with a mixture of awe and reverence. These were the most powerful and respected members of the Phoenix Kingdom, each one a master of the fire arts, and each one deeply connected to the elemental forces that governed their world. They had been preparing for this moment their entire lives, knowing that they would witness the birth of a king who would shape the future of Eldoria.

The High Priestess, a woman of remarkable beauty and wisdom, stepped forward, her robes flowing around her like liquid fire. Her hair, a cascade of fiery red, seemed to move with a life of its own, and her eyes burned with the light of the Sacred Flame. She raised her hands to the sky and began to chant in the ancient tongue, her voice resonating with power as she called upon the gods to bless the birth of the Phoenix King.

As the chant echoed through the night, the Sacred Flame roared to life, its flames growing higher and higher until they reached the sky. The ground trembled beneath the Fireborn's feet, and the air crackled with energy, a tangible force that made the hairs on their arms stand on end. The Fireborn watched in awe as the flames began to swirl, forming a vortex of fire that pulsed with an otherworldly intensity.

From the heart of the Sacred Flame, a shape began to emerge—a silhouette of pure light, growing clearer with each passing moment. The Fireborn gasped as they saw the figure taking form, its outline glowing with the radiant light of the flames. It was the shape of a phoenix, but not just any phoenix—this was the Phoenix King, the one foretold by the prophecy.

As the figure stepped forward, it became clear that this was no ordinary being. The flames seemed to cling to the figure, wrapping around it like a cloak, and as it emerged fully from the fire, the Fireborn fell to their knees in reverence. Before them stood a phoenix unlike any they had ever seen—a creature of unparalleled beauty and power, its feathers a shimmering blend of gold and red, each one glowing with an inner light that seemed to pulse with life.

The phoenix's eyes were like twin suns, burning with an intensity that seemed to pierce through the very soul. As it spread its wings, the air shimmered with heat, and the Fireborn could feel the power emanating from the creature—a power that was both terrifying and awe-inspiring. This was the Phoenix King, the one born from the purest flame, the one destined to bring balance to Eldoria.

The Phoenix King let out a cry, a sound that echoed through the night and resonated with the very essence of the Fireborn. It was a call that spoke of power, of destiny, and of the eternal cycle of life and death. The Fireborn knew that this was the moment they had been waiting for, the moment that would change the course of their history.

As the Phoenix King stood before the Sacred Flame, the High Priestess stepped forward, her eyes locked on the magnificent creature before her. She bowed deeply, her voice filled with reverence as she spoke the ancient words of greeting, words that had not been spoken since the time of the first Phoenix King.

"Great Phoenix King," she intoned, her voice trembling with emotion, "you have been born from the purest flame, as foretold by the prophecy. You are the one destined to bring balance to our world, to guide us through the trials that lie ahead, and to lead us into a new era of peace and prosperity. We pledge our loyalty to you, our king, and we offer our lives in service to your cause."

The Phoenix King regarded the High Priestess with eyes that seemed to see into her very soul. For a moment, the world seemed to stand still, the only sound the crackling of the Sacred Flame. Then, the Phoenix King lowered its head in acknowledgment, a gesture that sent a wave of relief and joy through the gathered Fireborn.

The High Priestess rose to her feet, her heart swelling with pride and hope. She knew that the birth of the Phoenix King marked the beginning of a new era for the Phoenix Kingdom, an era that would be defined by the prophecy and the destiny that lay before them. But she also knew that the journey ahead would be fraught with challenges, that the Phoenix King would face enemies both old and new, and that the balance they sought to achieve would come at a great cost.

As the Fireborn celebrated the birth of their new king, the Phoenix King spread its wings and took to the sky, its form illuminated by the light of the Sacred Flame. The sight of the majestic creature soaring above them filled the Fireborn with a sense of awe and wonder, and they knew that they were witnessing the beginning of a legend.

The Phoenix King circled above the Sacred Flame, its cry echoing through the night as it surveyed the land that was now its domain. It was a sight that would be etched into the memories of the Fireborn for generations to come, a symbol of hope and resilience, of power and wisdom.

The Prophecy and the Destiny

The birth of the Phoenix King was more than just the arrival of a new ruler—it was the fulfillment of an ancient prophecy that had been passed down through the ages. The prophecy spoke of a time when the balance of Eldoria would be shattered, when darkness would threaten to consume the land, and when the elemental forces would be thrown into chaos.

In this time of great turmoil, the prophecy foretold, a Phoenix King would rise—a king born from the purest flame, with the power to restore balance to the world. This Phoenix King would be the embodiment of the Eternal Flame, a being of light and fire, destined to guide the world through its darkest hour and lead it into a new era of harmony.

But the prophecy also spoke of great challenges, of battles to be fought, and sacrifices to be made. The Phoenix King would face enemies that sought to destroy him, forces that would stop at nothing to upset the balance and plunge Eldoria into eternal night. The journey ahead would be one of fire and ash, of destruction and renewal, of light and darkness.

The Fireborn knew that their new king would need to harness the power of the Eternal Flame, to master the ancient arts of fire, and to confront the darkness that threatened their world. They also knew that the Phoenix King's journey would not be one that he could undertake alone—he would need the support of his people, the wisdom of the elders, and the guidance of the elemental forces that governed their world.

As the Phoenix King descended from the sky and landed before the Sacred Flame, the High Priestess approached him, her heart heavy with the knowledge of the prophecy. She knew that the path before them would be difficult, that the Phoenix King would face trials unlike any before, and that the future of their world rested in his hands.

"Great Phoenix King," she began, her voice filled with a mixture of pride and trepidation, "the prophecy has foretold your arrival, and with it, the challenges that you must face. You are the one destined to restore balance to our world, to guide us through the darkness and into the light. But know this—your journey will not be easy. The forces that seek to destroy us are powerful, and they will stop at nothing to see you fail."

The Phoenix King regarded the High Priestess with a calm, unwavering gaze. He knew the weight of the prophecy, the expectations that had been placed upon him, and the challenges that lay ahead. But he also knew that he had been born for this purpose, that his destiny was to fulfill the prophecy and bring balance to Eldoria.

"I understand," the Phoenix King replied, his voice resonating with the power of the flames. "I was born from the purest flame, and I will use the power of the Eternal Flame to fulfill the prophecy and restore balance to our world. But I will not do this alone. I will need the support of the Fireborn, the wisdom of the elders, and the guidance of the elemental forces that govern our land."

The High Priestess nodded, her heart swelling with pride and hope. She knew that the Phoenix King was the one foretold by the prophecy, the one who could lead them through the trials ahead and bring about the renewal that Eldoria so desperately needed.

With the birth of the Phoenix King, the prophecy had been set in motion, and the world of Eldoria would never be the same again. The forces of darkness were already stirring, awakened by the arrival of the prophesied king, and the balance of the world hung in the balance.

But the Phoenix King was ready. With the power of the Eternal Flame at his command, and the support of his people behind him, he would face whatever challenges lay ahead. The journey would be difficult, and the sacrifices great, but the Phoenix King knew that his destiny was to fulfill the prophecy and bring balance to the world.

The Sacred Oath

As the Phoenix King stood before the Sacred Flame, the Fireborn gathered around him, their hearts filled with a mixture of hope and determination. They knew that the road ahead would be fraught with challenges, that the forces arrayed against them were formidable, but they also knew that they had a king who was destined to lead them to victory.

The High Priestess stepped forward, her voice clear and strong as she addressed the gathered Fireborn. "On this night, we bear witness to the birth of the Phoenix King, the one foretold by the prophecy. He is our hope, our light in the darkness, and the one who will restore balance to our world. But he cannot do this alone. It is up to us, the Fireborn, to stand by his side, to support him in his journey, and to ensure that the prophecy is fulfilled."

The Fireborn raised their voices in agreement, their words echoing through the night as they pledged their loyalty to their new king. They knew that they were part of something greater than themselves, that they were the protectors of the flame, the guardians of the balance, and the ones who would ensure the survival of their world.

The High Priestess turned to the Phoenix King, her eyes filled with pride and determination. "Great Phoenix King, we, the Fireborn, pledge our loyalty to you. We offer our lives in service to your cause, and we vow to stand by your side as you fulfill the prophecy and restore balance to our world. Together, we will face the challenges ahead, and together, we will emerge victorious."

The Phoenix King lowered his head in acknowledgment, a gesture that sent a wave of relief and joy through the gathered Fireborn. He knew that he was not alone in his journey, that he had the support of his people, the wisdom of the elders, and the power of the Eternal Flame at his command.

As the Fireborn celebrated the birth of their new king, the Phoenix King spread his wings and took to the sky, his form illuminated by the light of the Sacred Flame. The sight of the majestic creature soaring above them filled the Fireborn with a sense of awe and wonder, and they knew that they were witnessing the beginning of a legend.

The Phoenix King circled above the Sacred Flame, his cry echoing through the night as he surveyed the land that was now his domain. It was a sight that would be etched into the memories of the Fireborn for generations to come, a symbol of hope and resilience, of power and wisdom.

The Journey Begins

With the birth of the Phoenix King, the prophecy had been set in motion, and the world of Eldoria would never be the same again. The forces of darkness were already stirring, awakened by the arrival of the prophesied king, and the balance of the world hung in the balance.

But the Phoenix King was ready. With the power of the Eternal Flame at his command, and the support of his people behind him, he would face whatever challenges lay ahead. The journey would be difficult, and the sacrifices great, but the Phoenix King knew that his destiny was to fulfill the prophecy and bring balance to the world.

As the Phoenix King descended from the sky and landed before the Sacred Flame, the Fireborn gathered around him, their hearts filled with a mixture of hope and determination. They knew that the road ahead would be fraught with challenges, that the forces arrayed against them were formidable, but they also knew that they had a king who was destined to lead them to victory.

The High Priestess stepped forward, her voice clear and strong as she addressed the gathered Fireborn. "On this night, we bear witness to the birth of the Phoenix King, the one foretold by the prophecy. He is our hope, our light in the darkness, and the one who will restore balance to our world. But he cannot do this alone. It is up to us, the Fireborn, to stand by his side, to support him in his journey, and to ensure that the prophecy is fulfilled."

The Fireborn raised their voices in agreement, their words echoing through the night as they pledged their loyalty to their new king. They knew that they were part of something greater than themselves, that they were the protectors of the flame, the guardians of the balance, and the ones who would ensure the survival of their world.

The High Priestess turned to the Phoenix King, her eyes filled with pride and determination. "Great Phoenix King, we, the Fireborn, pledge our loyalty to you. We offer our lives in service to your cause, and we vow to stand by your side as you fulfill the prophecy and restore balance to our world. Together, we will face the challenges ahead, and together, we will emerge victorious."

The Phoenix King lowered his head in acknowledgment, a gesture that sent a wave of relief and joy through the gathered Fireborn. He knew that he was not alone in his journey, that he had the support of his people, the wisdom of the elders, and the power of the Eternal Flame at his command.

As the Fireborn celebrated the birth of their new king, the Phoenix King spread his wings and took to the sky, his form illuminated by the light of the Sacred Flame. The sight of the majestic creature soaring above them filled the Fireborn with a sense of awe and wonder, and they knew that they were witnessing the beginning of a legend.

The Phoenix King circled above the Sacred Flame, his cry echoing through the night as he surveyed the land that was now his domain. It was a sight that would be etched into the memories of the Fireborn for generations to come, a symbol of hope and resilience, of power and wisdom.

The Beginning of a Legend

The legend of the Phoenix King had begun, a tale of a king born from fire, destined to rise from the ashes and bring balance to a world on the brink of destruction. It was a story that would be told for generations, a story of hope and sacrifice, of power and wisdom. The world of Eldoria would never be the same, for the Phoenix King had risen, and with him came the promise of a brighter future.

As the Phoenix King took flight, his wings glowing with the light of the Eternal Flame, the Fireborn watched in awe, their hearts filled with pride and determination. They knew that they were part of something greater than themselves, that they were the guardians of the flame, the protectors of the balance, and the ones who would ensure the survival of their world.

The Phoenix King soared above the Phoenix Kingdom, his eyes taking in the land that was now his to protect. He could see the towering volcanoes, the rivers of molten lava, and the glowing Emberblooms that dotted the landscape. He could feel the power of the Eternal Flame coursing through him, a power that connected him to the very essence of Eldoria.

But he also knew that the journey ahead would be difficult, that the forces arrayed against him were formidable, and that the balance they sought to achieve would come at a great cost. The Phoenix King was ready for the challenges that lay ahead, and he knew that he had the support of his people, the wisdom of the elders, and the guidance of the elemental forces that governed their world.

As the Phoenix King flew over the land, he could feel the eyes of the Fireborn upon him, their hearts filled with hope and determination. He knew that they were counting on him to fulfill the prophecy, to bring balance to their world, and to lead them into a new era of peace and prosperity.

The Phoenix King let out a cry, a sound that echoed through the night and resonated with the very essence of the Fireborn. It was a call that spoke of power, of destiny, and of the eternal cycle of life and death. The Fireborn knew that this was the moment they had been waiting for, the moment that would change the course of their history.

As the Phoenix King continued his flight, he knew that his journey had just begun. The challenges ahead would be great, the enemies formidable, but he was ready. With the power of the Eternal Flame at his command, and the support of his people behind him, he would face whatever challenges lay ahead.

The legend of the Phoenix King had begun, and the world of Eldoria would never be the same again. The forces of darkness were already stirring, awakened by the arrival of the prophesied king, and the balance of the world hung in the balance.

But the Phoenix King was ready. With the power of the Eternal Flame at his command, and the support of his people behind him, he would face whatever challenges lay ahead. The journey would be difficult, and the sacrifices great, but the Phoenix King knew that his destiny was to fulfill the prophecy and bring balance to the world.

And so, the Phoenix King soared into the night, his fiery form lighting up the sky. The prophecy had been set in motion, the forces of darkness were stirring, and the balance of Eldoria hung in the balance. But the Phoenix King was ready, and with the power of the Eternal Flame, he would face whatever challenges lay ahead.

The legend of the Phoenix King had begun, and the world of Eldoria would never be the same again.

Chapter 2: The Flame's Embrace

The Early Years: A Childhood of Fire

The Phoenix King was born in the heart of the Sacred Flame, but his life, like that of any other being, began with the innocence of childhood. Though he was destined to be a ruler, a savior, and a beacon of hope for his people, the early years of his life were filled with the wonders of discovery and the challenges of understanding his unique place in the world.

In the Phoenix Kingdom, the fire was not simply a source of warmth or a tool for cooking—it was a living force, a constant presence that shaped every aspect of life. The Phoenix King's childhood was spent learning to understand and embrace the fire, to see it not just as a force of nature but as an extension of his very being. From the moment he first opened his eyes, the flames were his constant companions, their warmth a comforting embrace and their light a guiding force.

As a young phoenix, the Phoenix King was curious and adventurous, always eager to explore the world around him. The Sacred Flame, where he had been born, was his first playground, and he would spend hours soaring through its glowing tendrils, feeling the heat on his feathers and the energy coursing through his body. The fire was alive, responding to his every movement, and he quickly learned that he could control it, bending it to his will with just a thought.

But the fire was also a teacher, and it had many lessons to impart. The Phoenix King's childhood was not without its challenges, for the fire was a demanding master. It required focus, discipline, and respect. There were times when the flames would lash out at him, testing his resolve and his ability to control his powers. He would feel the searing heat on his skin, the sting of the fire's touch, and he would be reminded that, while he was born from the flames, he was not immune to their wrath.

The Phoenix King's early lessons were often harsh, but they were necessary. He learned that fire could be both a friend and a foe, a force of creation and destruction. He learned to respect its power, to understand its dual nature, and to harness it in a way that would benefit not just himself but his entire kingdom.

These lessons would become the foundation of his rule, guiding him in his future decisions as he sought to bring balance to his world.

The people of the Phoenix Kingdom watched as their young king grew, marveling at his natural affinity for fire and his remarkable abilities. They saw in him the potential for greatness, the promise of a ruler who would lead them into a new era of prosperity. But they also knew that he would need guidance, that his raw power needed to be tempered with wisdom and knowledge.

The Arrival of the Mentor

When the Phoenix King reached the age where he could begin to comprehend the deeper mysteries of fire, the elders of the Phoenix Kingdom knew it was time for him to meet his mentor. This mentor was not just any phoenix—he was an ancient and wise being, one of the first to be born from the Sacred Flame, and he had lived for countless centuries. His name was Ignatius, and he was revered throughout the Phoenix Kingdom for his knowledge of the ancient laws of fire and resurrection.

Ignatius was a massive phoenix, his feathers a deep, iridescent crimson that shimmered with shades of gold and amber. His eyes, the color of molten lava, held the wisdom of ages, and his presence commanded respect. When he arrived at the Sacred Flame to begin his tutelage of the young Phoenix King, the entire kingdom fell silent, their eyes fixed on the ancient bird.

The first meeting between the Phoenix King and Ignatius was a momentous occasion, one that would shape the future of the kingdom. The young king, though confident in his abilities, felt a deep sense of awe as he stood before the ancient phoenix. Ignatius regarded him with a penetrating gaze, as if assessing the very essence of his being. For a long moment, neither of them spoke, the only sound the crackling of the Sacred Flame.

Finally, Ignatius lowered his head in a gesture of acknowledgment. "Young king," he began, his voice deep and resonant, "you have been born from the purest flame, destined to lead our people and bring balance to the world. But power alone is not enough. To fulfill your destiny, you must learn the ancient ways, the laws that govern the fire and the cycle of life and death. I am here to teach you, to guide you on your journey, and to prepare you for the challenges that lie ahead."

The Phoenix King bowed his head in respect, understanding the gravity of the moment. "I am honored, Master Ignatius," he replied, his voice steady despite the nervous excitement he felt. "I am ready to learn, to embrace the knowledge you have to offer."

And so began the Phoenix King's training under Ignatius, a rigorous and demanding process that would last for many years. Ignatius was a strict but fair teacher, pushing the young king to his limits and beyond. He taught him not just how to control the fire, but how to understand it on a fundamental level, to see it as a living force with its own will and purpose.

One of the first lessons Ignatius imparted was the concept of balance. "Fire is both a creator and a destroyer," he explained as they stood before the Sacred Flame. "It gives life by providing warmth and light, but it can also take life by consuming everything in its path. As the Phoenix King, you must learn to wield this power with care. You must understand when to let the fire burn and when to extinguish it. This is the essence of balance, and it is the foundation of your rule."

The Phoenix King listened intently, absorbing every word. He practiced day and night, honing his skills and deepening his understanding of the fire. Ignatius would often take him to the far reaches of the Phoenix Kingdom, to the tops of volcanoes where the lava flowed freely, or to the deepest caverns where the earth was still molten. In these places, the Phoenix King learned to connect with the fire on a deeper level, to feel its pulse in the land and to channel its energy through his own body.

But Ignatius' teachings were not limited to the physical aspects of fire. He also delved into the spiritual and philosophical dimensions, teaching the Phoenix King about the cycle of life, death, and rebirth. "Just as a phoenix rises from its ashes, so too does the world cycle through periods of destruction and renewal," Ignatius explained one evening as they sat by a lava lake, its glowing surface casting an eerie light on their feathers. "This cycle is necessary for growth and transformation. As the Phoenix King, you are the guardian of this cycle. You must ensure that the world does not fall into stagnation, that it continues to evolve and thrive."

The Phoenix King pondered these words, understanding the weight of the responsibility that rested on his shoulders. He knew that his role was not just to lead his people, but to guide the world through its cycles, to maintain the balance between life and death, creation and destruction. This understanding began to shape his view of the world, influencing his decisions and actions as he grew into his role as king.

The Fire Spirit's Visit

As the Phoenix King continued his training, he began to experience visions—flashes of light, whispers in the wind, and a sense of something greater calling out to him. These visions became more frequent and more intense as time went on, and though he did not fully understand them, he felt that they were leading him towards something important.

One night, as the Phoenix King lay by the Sacred Flame, his mind was filled with a particularly vivid vision. He saw himself standing in the heart of a great fire, surrounded by flames that danced and flickered with a life of their own. In the center of the fire, a figure began to take shape—a being made entirely of flame, its form shifting and flowing like liquid fire. The figure approached him, its presence both awe-inspiring and terrifying.

"Young king," the figure spoke, its voice echoing with the power of the fire itself, "I am the Fire Spirit, the essence of the Eternal Flame that burns at the heart of your world. I have watched over you since your birth, and I have seen the path you walk. The time has come for you to learn the secrets of the Immortal Fire, the source of your power and the key to fulfilling your destiny."

The Phoenix King stared in awe at the Fire Spirit, feeling its energy radiating through him. "I am honored by your presence, great spirit," he replied, his voice trembling with a mixture of excitement and fear. "But I do not fully understand—what is the Immortal Fire, and how can I harness its power?"

The Fire Spirit's form flickered, the flames around it flaring with intensity. "The Immortal Fire is the source of all life, the spark that ignites the cycle of creation and destruction. It is the fire that burns within you, the fire that connects you to the Sacred Flame and to the very essence of the world. To harness its power, you must first understand it, and to understand it, you must embark on a journey of self-discovery and enlightenment."

The Phoenix King listened intently, his mind racing with questions. "But how do I begin this journey?" he asked, his voice filled with determination. "How do I learn the secrets of the Immortal Fire?"

The Fire Spirit regarded him with what seemed to be a smile, though its form was ever-shifting, making it difficult to tell. "The journey begins within," it replied, its voice softening. "You must look deep into your own soul, confront your fears and doubts, and embrace the fire that burns within you. Only then can you truly understand the power of the Immortal Fire and use it to fulfill your destiny."

The Phoenix King nodded, determination and resolve filling his heart. "I will do as you say," he vowed, his voice steady. "I will embark on this journey, and I will learn the secrets of the Immortal Fire."

The Fire Spirit seemed pleased with his response, and it began to fade, its form dissolving into the flames that surrounded it. "Remember, young king," it whispered as it disappeared, "the fire is both your greatest ally and your greatest challenge. Embrace it, and it will guide you to your destiny."

As the vision faded, the Phoenix King awoke, the words of the Fire Spirit still echoing in his mind. He knew that his journey was far from over, that the road ahead would be filled with challenges and trials, but he also knew that he had been given a glimpse of the power that awaited him. The Immortal Fire was the key to his destiny, and he was determined to unlock its secrets.

Embracing the Immortal Fire

The Phoenix King wasted no time in beginning his journey of self-discovery. Under the guidance of Ignatius, he delved deeper into the mysteries of fire, exploring not just its physical properties but its spiritual and metaphysical dimensions as well. He meditated by the Sacred Flame, seeking to connect with the fire on a deeper level, to understand its essence and its role in the cycle of life and death.

Ignatius, recognizing the importance of the Phoenix King's journey, provided him with the tools and knowledge he needed to succeed. He taught the young king the ancient rituals of fire, ceremonies that had been passed down through generations of phoenixes, each one designed to strengthen the connection between the phoenix and the fire. These rituals were often complex and demanding, requiring immense focus and concentration, but the Phoenix King embraced them wholeheartedly, knowing that they were essential to his growth and understanding.

One of the most important rituals was the Rite of Embers, a ceremony that involved immersing oneself in the flames of the Sacred Flame, allowing the fire to cleanse and purify the soul. The Phoenix King performed this ritual regularly, each time emerging from the flames with a deeper understanding of his own power and the role he was destined to play in the world.

But the journey was not without its challenges. The Phoenix King often found himself struggling to balance the dual nature of fire—the creative and destructive forces that existed within him. There were moments when the fire threatened to consume him, to overwhelm his senses and drive him to the brink of madness. In these moments, he would hear the words of the Fire Spirit, reminding him to embrace the fire, to see it as both a challenge and a guide.

As the years passed, the Phoenix King's connection to the fire grew stronger, and with it, his understanding of the Immortal Fire deepened. He began to see the fire not just as a force of nature, but as a living, breathing entity, one that was intimately connected to the very fabric of existence. He realized that the fire was a reflection of his own soul, that the flames that burned within him were a manifestation of the eternal cycle of life and death, creation and destruction.

Ignatius watched with pride as the Phoenix King continued to grow, knowing that he was on the right path. But he also knew that the journey was far from over, that there were still many challenges to be faced, and that the Phoenix King would need to be prepared for the trials that lay ahead.

One day, as they stood together on the edge of a volcano, watching the lava flow beneath them, Ignatius turned to the Phoenix King, his eyes filled with wisdom and concern. "You have come far, young king," he said, his voice gentle yet firm. "But there is still much you must learn. The fire within you is powerful, but it is also dangerous. You must continue to seek balance, to understand the dual nature of the flames, and to use your power wisely."

The Phoenix King nodded, understanding the gravity of Ignatius' words. "I will continue to learn," he vowed, his voice filled with determination. "I will embrace the fire within me, and I will use it to fulfill my destiny."

Ignatius smiled, a rare expression on his ancient face. "I have no doubt that you will succeed," he replied, his voice filled with confidence. "But remember this, young king—power is not just about strength or control. It is also about wisdom, compassion, and understanding. As you continue on your journey, do not lose sight of these qualities, for they are just as important as the fire that burns within you."

The Phoenix King took Ignatius' words to heart, knowing that they held a deeper truth. He understood that his journey was not just about mastering his powers, but also about becoming the kind of leader his people needed—a leader who was strong, wise, and compassionate, who could guide them through the challenges ahead and bring balance to their world.

As the Phoenix King continued his training, he began to experience a new kind of connection with the fire—a connection that went beyond the physical and the spiritual. He began to feel the fire as a part of himself, as an extension of his own soul. He could sense its presence in the world around him, in the flames of the Sacred Flame, in the molten lava that flowed through the land, and even in the hearts of his people.

This connection to the fire gave the Phoenix King a new sense of purpose and responsibility. He knew that he was not just a ruler, but a guardian of the flame, a protector of the balance between creation and destruction. He understood that his role was not just to lead his people, but to guide them through the cycles of life and death, to ensure that the world continued to evolve and thrive.

The Phoenix King's understanding of the Immortal Fire continued to deepen, and with it, his powers grew. He found that he could summon flames with just a thought, could control the intensity and direction of the fire, and could even use it to heal wounds and restore life. He began to see the fire as a tool, a force that he could use to shape the world around him, to create and to destroy, to give life and to take it away.

But with this power came a sense of caution and responsibility. The Phoenix King knew that the fire was a dangerous force, one that could easily spiral out of control if not used wisely. He understood that his role was not just to wield the fire, but to protect it, to ensure that it was used for the greater good, and to prevent it from becoming a force of destruction.

Ignatius continued to guide the Phoenix King, teaching him the ancient laws of fire and resurrection, imparting the wisdom of ages. The Phoenix King listened intently, knowing that these lessons were essential to his growth and understanding. He knew that he was being prepared for something greater, something that would test his powers and his resolve in ways he could not yet imagine.

The First Trial

As the Phoenix King's training continued, Ignatius began to speak of a trial—a test that every Phoenix King must undergo, a rite of passage that would determine whether he was truly ready to fulfill his destiny. This trial was known as the Trial of Ashes, and it was said to be the ultimate test of a phoenix's strength, wisdom, and understanding of the fire.

"The Trial of Ashes is not just a test of your physical abilities," Ignatius explained one evening as they sat by the Sacred Flame. "It is a test of your soul, of your understanding of the fire and the balance it represents. You will be faced with challenges that will push you to your limits, that will force you to confront your deepest fears and doubts. Only by overcoming these challenges will you prove yourself worthy of the title of Phoenix King."

The Phoenix King listened with a mixture of anticipation and trepidation. He knew that the Trial of Ashes was a necessary step in his journey, but he also knew that it would be the most difficult challenge he had ever faced. "What must I do to prepare for the trial?" he asked, his voice filled with determination.

Ignatius regarded him with a calm, steady gaze. "You must continue to train, to deepen your understanding of the fire and the balance it represents. But more than that, you must look within yourself, to confront the darkness that resides within you, to embrace the fire that burns in your soul. Only then will you be ready to face the Trial of Ashes."

The Phoenix King nodded, understanding the gravity of the task before him. He knew that the Trial of Ashes would not just test his powers, but his very soul, and he was determined to be ready for whatever challenges lay ahead.

As the day of the trial approached, the Phoenix King devoted himself entirely to his training. He spent hours meditating by the Sacred Flame, seeking to connect with the fire on a deeper level, to understand its essence and its role in the cycle of life and death. He practiced the ancient rituals that Ignatius had taught him, honing his skills and deepening his connection to the fire.

The Fireborn watched in awe as their young king prepared for the trial, knowing that he was about to undergo a test that would determine the future of their kingdom. They offered their support and their prayers, knowing that the Phoenix King's success was not just a personal victory, but a victory for the entire kingdom.

Finally, the day of the trial arrived. The Phoenix King stood before the Sacred Flame, his heart filled with a mixture of anticipation and resolve. He knew that the Trial of Ashes would be the ultimate test of his abilities, but he also knew that he was ready, that he had been prepared for this moment his entire life.

Ignatius stood beside him, his eyes filled with pride and confidence. "Remember, young king," he said, his voice gentle yet firm, "the fire is both your greatest ally and your greatest challenge. Embrace it, and it will guide you through the trial. Trust in your abilities, trust in the fire, and you will emerge victorious."

The Phoenix King nodded, taking a deep breath as he prepared to step into the flames. He knew that the Trial of Ashes would be the most difficult challenge he had ever faced, but he also knew that he was ready, that he had the strength, the wisdom, and the understanding to succeed.

As he stepped into the flames, the world around him seemed to disappear, replaced by the searing heat and the blinding light of the fire. He could feel the flames consuming him, burning away his fears and doubts, leaving only the pure essence of his soul.

The trial had begun, and the Phoenix King was ready.

The Fire Within

The Trial of Ashes was unlike anything the Phoenix King had ever experienced. The flames surrounded him, their heat intense and all-consuming, but instead of pain, he felt a strange sense of clarity and focus. The fire was not just burning his body—it was burning away his doubts, his fears, and his weaknesses, leaving only the essence of his soul.

As he stood in the heart of the flames, the Phoenix King began to see visions—images of his past, his present, and his future. He saw himself as a young phoenix, learning to control his powers, struggling to understand the dual nature of the fire. He saw the faces of the Fireborn, his people, looking to him for guidance and leadership. And he saw the future, a future filled with challenges and trials, but also with hope and promise.

But the visions were not just of himself. The Phoenix King saw the world of Eldoria, the elemental forces that governed it, and the delicate balance that held everything together. He saw the fire as a living force, a force that was both a creator and a destroyer, a force that could bring life and death in equal measure. He understood that his role as the Phoenix King was not just to wield this power, but to protect it, to ensure that it was used wisely and for the greater good.

The flames around him intensified, and the Phoenix King could feel the fire testing him, pushing him to his limits. He could feel the darkness within him, the doubts and fears that had haunted him for so long, rising to the surface. But instead of succumbing to them, he embraced them, accepting them as part of himself, as part of the balance that he was destined to protect.

In that moment, the Phoenix King felt a surge of power unlike anything he had ever experienced. The fire within him, the Immortal Fire that connected him to the Sacred Flame, flared to life, filling him with a sense of purpose and determination. He understood now that the fire was not just a tool or a weapon—it was a part of him, a reflection of his own soul.

As the flames began to recede, the Phoenix King emerged from the Trial of Ashes, his feathers glowing with a radiant light. He felt stronger, wiser, and more connected to the fire than ever before. He knew that he had passed the trial, that he had proven himself worthy of the title of Phoenix King.

Ignatius watched with pride as the Phoenix King emerged from the flames, knowing that he had succeeded in his journey. "You have done well, young king," he said, his voice filled with admiration. "You have embraced the fire within you, and in doing so, you have unlocked the true power of the Immortal Fire. You are ready to fulfill your destiny, to lead our people, and to bring balance to our world."

The Phoenix King nodded, his heart filled with a sense of accomplishment and purpose. He knew that his journey was far from over, that there were still many challenges ahead, but he also knew that he was ready to face them. He had embraced the fire within him, and he was determined to use its power to protect his people and to fulfill the prophecy.

As the Phoenix King stood before the Sacred Flame, his eyes filled with determination, he knew that he was not just a ruler—he was a guardian of the flame, a protector of the balance, and a beacon of hope for his people. The fire had tested him, had pushed him to his limits, but it had also shaped him, had made him the king he was destined to be.

The legend of the Phoenix King had truly begun, and the world of Eldoria would never be the same again.

Chapter 3: The Trial of Ashes

The Prelude to the Trial

The Trial of Ashes was an ancient rite, an ordeal that every Phoenix King had to face to prove their worthiness to rule. It was not merely a test of physical strength or magical prowess, but a profound examination of the soul—a journey into the heart of the fire, where one's deepest fears and greatest challenges were laid bare. The Phoenix King had trained for this moment under the guidance of Ignatius, but even with all his preparation, he knew that nothing could truly ready him for what he was about to face.

The morning of the trial dawned with a sky tinged in hues of red and orange, as if the very heavens were ablaze. The air was thick with anticipation, and the entire Phoenix Kingdom seemed to hold its breath. The Sacred Flame, ever-burning at the heart of the kingdom, crackled with a renewed intensity, as if aware of the momentous event that was about to unfold.

The Fireborn, the people of the Phoenix Kingdom, gathered around the Sacred Flame, their faces a mixture of reverence and concern. They had seen many Phoenix Kings undergo the Trial of Ashes, and they knew the dangers it posed. Some had emerged victorious, strengthened by the ordeal, while others had been consumed by the fire, their reigns cut tragically short. The stakes were high, for the trial would determine whether the young Phoenix King was truly the one foretold by the prophecy—the one who would bring balance to Eldoria.

Ignatius, the ancient and wise phoenix who had been the Phoenix King's mentor, stood by his side. His deep, molten eyes reflected the flames, and his voice was calm but firm as he spoke. "Today, you will face the Trial of Ashes, the rite that has tested every Phoenix King before you. It will not be easy. The fire will challenge you, will push you to the brink of your endurance, but you must endure. Remember the lessons you have learned. Remember the balance between creation and destruction, life and death. Only by embracing the fire and understanding its dual nature will you succeed."

The Phoenix King nodded, his heart pounding with a mixture of anticipation and fear. He knew the trial would test him in ways he could not yet comprehend, but he was determined to prove himself worthy of the title of Phoenix King. "I am ready, Master Ignatius," he said, his voice steady despite the turmoil within him. "I will face the fire, and I will emerge victorious."

Ignatius regarded him with a solemn expression. "You have the strength within you, young king. Trust in yourself, trust in the fire, and trust in the journey ahead. The flames will show you the way."

With those final words, Ignatius stepped back, leaving the Phoenix King to face the trial alone. The gathered Fireborn watched in silence as the young king approached the Sacred Flame, the fire that had given birth to him and that would now test his very soul.

The Phoenix King took a deep breath, feeling the heat of the flames on his skin, the crackle of the fire in his ears. He knew that this moment would define his reign, that the trial would determine whether he was truly worthy to lead his people. With a final glance at the Fireborn, he stepped into the Sacred Flame, his heart filled with resolve.

Entering the Flames

As the Phoenix King stepped into the Sacred Flame, the world around him seemed to dissolve into an inferno of light and heat. The flames engulfed him, their intensity overwhelming, but instead of pain, he felt a strange sense of clarity. The fire was not merely consuming him—it was transforming him, stripping away the layers of his being, revealing the essence of his soul.

The Trial of Ashes had begun.

The Phoenix King felt himself descending into the heart of the fire, the flames swirling around him in a dance of destruction and creation. He could no longer see the gathered Fireborn, no longer hear the crackle of the Sacred Flame. All that existed was the fire, and within it, he could sense a presence—something ancient and powerful, watching him, judging him.

As he continued to descend, the flames began to take shape, forming visions that played out before his eyes. The first vision was of the past—of the Phoenix Kings who had come before him. He saw their faces, their eyes burning with the light of the fire, their wings outstretched as they soared through the skies of Eldoria. Each one had faced the Trial of Ashes, had undergone the same test of fire and spirit, and each one had left a mark on the history of the Phoenix Kingdom.

The Phoenix King watched as the visions unfolded, showing him the triumphs and tragedies of those who had come before. He saw Phoenix Kings who had brought great prosperity to the kingdom, who had used their powers to protect their people and ensure the balance of the world. But he also saw those who had faltered, who had been consumed by the fire, their reigns ending in flames and ash.

The visions were both inspiring and sobering. The Phoenix King felt the weight of his heritage, the responsibility that came with being a Phoenix King. He knew that he was part of a long line of rulers, each one tasked with maintaining the balance between life and death, creation and destruction. But he also knew that the trial was not just about living up to the legacy of those who had come before—it was about forging his own path, proving himself worthy of the title he bore.

As the visions of past Phoenix Kings faded, the flames around him grew darker, more intense. The Phoenix King felt a surge of energy, a force that seemed to resonate with the fire within him. He knew that the next part of the trial was about to begin, and he braced himself for what was to come.

The Visions of Sacrifice

The flames around the Phoenix King began to shift once more, and he found himself standing in a vast, barren landscape, the ground scorched and lifeless. The air was heavy with the scent of ash, and the sky above was dark, devoid of stars or light. It was a desolate place, a place where the fire had burned everything to the ground, leaving only destruction in its wake.

As the Phoenix King looked around, he saw figures emerging from the shadows—figures of Phoenix Kings long past, their forms flickering like flames in the darkness. Each one bore the scars of battle, the marks of sacrifice, and as they approached, the Phoenix King could feel their sorrow, their pain.

One of the figures stepped forward, its face etched with lines of age and wisdom. "We are the Phoenix Kings who have come before you," it said, its voice a deep, resonant echo. "We have ruled the Phoenix Kingdom, have faced the trials and challenges of our time, and have made the sacrifices necessary to maintain the balance of the world. Now, it is your turn."

The Phoenix King felt a chill run down his spine as the figure continued to speak. "To be a Phoenix King is to understand the importance of sacrifice. The fire is both a creator and a destroyer, and as its guardian, you must be willing to give of yourself, to endure the flames, to protect your people and your world. The balance of life and death, creation and destruction, rests upon your shoulders."

The Phoenix King nodded, understanding the gravity of the words. He had always known that being a Phoenix King required sacrifice, but now, standing before the figures of his predecessors, he could feel the weight of that responsibility more than ever.

The figures began to move closer, their forms flickering with intensity. "We will show you the sacrifices that must be made," the first figure said, its voice filled with a mix of sorrow and determination. "Only by understanding the true nature of sacrifice can you hope to pass the Trial of Ashes."

The Phoenix King braced himself as the figures surrounded him, the flames around them growing brighter. The visions began to unfold once more, showing him the sacrifices that had been made by the Phoenix Kings of the past.

He saw a young Phoenix King, his feathers still bright with the light of the fire, standing before his people as a great enemy approached. The Phoenix King could see the fear in the young ruler's eyes, but also the determination as he spread his wings and took to the sky, using his powers to hold back the enemy and protect his kingdom. But the battle was fierce, and in the end, the young Phoenix King was consumed by the flames, sacrificing himself to save his people.

The vision shifted, showing another Phoenix King, older and wiser, standing before the Sacred Flame. This king had ruled for many years, had brought peace and prosperity to the kingdom, but now, as his time drew near, he knew that he must pass on the mantle of leadership. The Phoenix King watched as the older ruler stepped into the flames, allowing the fire to consume him, to return him to the ashes from which he had been born. It was a sacrifice of self, a recognition of the cycle of life and death, of the need for renewal and rebirth.

The visions continued, each one showing a different Phoenix King, each one making a different sacrifice. Some sacrificed their lives, others their power, and others their very souls. But in each vision, the Phoenix King saw the same theme—the understanding that sacrifice was necessary to maintain the balance of the world, that the fire demanded both creation and destruction, life and death.

As the last vision faded, the Phoenix King found himself standing alone in the barren landscape, the figures of the past Phoenix Kings now gone. But their presence lingered, their words and their sacrifices etched into his mind.

He understood now what it meant to be a Phoenix King, what it meant to protect the balance of the world. The fire was not just a tool or a weapon—it was a living force, one that required sacrifice and understanding. The Phoenix King knew that he must be willing to make those sacrifices, to endure the flames, to protect his people and his world.

The Final Test

The landscape around the Phoenix King began to shift once more, the flames growing brighter, more intense. He could feel the fire closing in on him, the heat searing his feathers, but instead of fear, he felt a sense of resolve. He had seen the sacrifices of the past, had understood the importance of the balance between creation and destruction, and he was ready to face whatever challenge lay ahead.

The flames rose higher, forming a wall of fire around him. The heat was overwhelming, the light blinding, but the Phoenix King stood his ground, his heart filled with determination. He knew that this was the final test, the ultimate challenge of the Trial of Ashes.

As the flames closed in, the Phoenix King could feel the fire testing him, pushing him to his limits. He could feel the doubts and fears rising within him, the darkness that had haunted him for so long. But he also felt the strength of the fire within him, the Immortal Fire that connected him to the Sacred Flame, that gave him the power to endure.

The flames continued to rise, closing in on him, threatening to consume him. The Phoenix King could feel the heat searing his skin, the light blinding him, but he refused to back down. He knew that he had the strength within him, that he had the power to endure the flames and emerge victorious.

As the flames reached their peak, the Phoenix King closed his eyes, focusing on the fire within him. He could feel the Immortal Fire burning bright, giving him the strength and the resolve to face the final test. He understood now that the fire was not just a force of destruction—it was a force of renewal, of rebirth. It was the fire that gave life, that brought light to the darkness, that allowed the world to continue its eternal cycle.

With this understanding, the Phoenix King spread his wings, embracing the flames, allowing the fire to wash over him. He could feel the heat, the light, the power of the fire, but instead of pain, he felt a sense of peace, of clarity. The flames were not consuming him—they were transforming him, burning away the doubts and fears, leaving only the essence of his soul.

The Phoenix King felt a surge of power, the Immortal Fire within him flaring to life. He could feel the connection to the Sacred Flame, to the fire that burned at the heart of the world, and he knew that he had passed the final test. He had endured the flames, had faced his fears, had embraced the fire within him.

The flames began to recede, the light fading, the heat dissipating. The Phoenix King opened his eyes, his vision clearing, and he found himself standing once more before the Sacred Flame, the fire that had given birth to him and that had now tested his very soul.

Emerging Victorious

The Phoenix King stood before the Sacred Flame, his feathers glowing with a radiant light, his heart filled with a sense of accomplishment and purpose. He had faced the Trial of Ashes, had endured the flames, had understood the importance of sacrifice and the balance between creation and destruction. He knew now that he was ready to fulfill his destiny, to lead his people, and to bring balance to the world.

Ignatius, who had watched the trial from a distance, approached the Phoenix King, his eyes filled with pride and admiration. "You have done well, young king," he said, his voice resonating with warmth. "You have faced the

Trial of Ashes, have embraced the fire within you, and have proven yourself worthy of the title of Phoenix King."

The Phoenix King bowed his head in respect, his heart swelling with pride. "Thank you, Master Ignatius," he replied, his voice steady. "The trial was difficult, but it has shown me the true nature of the fire, the importance of sacrifice, and the balance that I must protect."

Ignatius nodded, his expression solemn. "The Trial of Ashes is not just a test of your abilities—it is a rite of passage, a journey into the heart of the fire. It has revealed to you the challenges you will face, the sacrifices you must be willing to make, and the power that lies within you. You are now ready to take your place as the rightful ruler of the Phoenix Kingdom."

The gathered Fireborn, who had watched the trial in silence, now erupted in cheers and applause, their voices filled with joy and relief. They had seen their young king emerge from the flames, had witnessed his strength and determination, and they knew that he was the one foretold by the prophecy—the one who would bring balance to their world.

The Phoenix King looked out at his people, his heart filled with a sense of unity and purpose. He knew that his journey was far from over, that there were still many challenges ahead, but he also knew that he had the strength and the wisdom to face them. He had earned his rightful place as the ruler of the Phoenix Kingdom, and he was determined to lead his people with the power of the fire and the knowledge of the balance.

As the Fireborn celebrated, the Phoenix King felt a sense of peace and fulfillment. He had passed the Trial of Ashes, had proven himself worthy, and had embraced the fire within him. The flames had tested him, had pushed him to his limits, but they had also shaped him, had made him the king he was destined to be.

The New Era

With the Trial of Ashes behind him, the Phoenix King was now fully recognized as the ruler of the Phoenix Kingdom. His people looked to him with reverence and trust, knowing that he had the strength, the wisdom, and the understanding to lead them through the challenges that lay ahead.

The Phoenix King took his place at the heart of the Phoenix Kingdom, standing before the Sacred Flame, the fire that had given birth to him and that would guide him in his reign. He knew that his role was not just to lead his people, but to protect the balance of the world, to ensure that the cycles of creation and destruction, life and death, continued in harmony.

He understood now that the fire was not just a tool or a weapon—it was a living force, one that required sacrifice and understanding. As the Phoenix King, he was the guardian of this fire, the protector of the balance, and the one who would guide his people through the cycles of life and death.

The Phoenix Kingdom entered a new era, one of prosperity and peace, guided by the wisdom and strength of their Phoenix King. The fire that burned at the heart of their world was now more than just a source of power—it was a symbol of unity, of resilience, and of the eternal cycle that connected all life in Eldoria.

The Phoenix King's reign would be long and prosperous, filled with challenges and triumphs, but he would always remember the lessons he had learned in the Trial of Ashes. He would remember the sacrifices of those who had come before him, the importance of balance, and the power of the fire within him.

And so, the Phoenix King took his place as the rightful ruler of the Phoenix Kingdom, his heart filled with resolve and purpose. The legend of the Phoenix King had truly begun, and the world of Eldoria would never be the same again.

Chapter 4: The Quest for the Eternal Flame

The Legend of the Eternal Flame

The Phoenix King had ruled the Phoenix Kingdom for several years now, and under his reign, the kingdom had thrived. The balance between creation and destruction, life and death, was carefully maintained, and the Fireborn, his people, had prospered. Yet, despite the peace and prosperity that had come to the Phoenix Kingdom, the Phoenix King knew that his journey was far from complete. The Trial of Ashes had been but the beginning—a test that had prepared him for the challenges to come. There was still much to learn, much to discover, and the Phoenix King's heart was restless with the knowledge that there was a greater destiny awaiting him.

In the depths of the Sacred Flame, where the Phoenix King often meditated, he had begun to experience visions—glimpses of a power far greater than any he had ever known. These visions spoke of the Eternal Flame, a source of unlimited power, said to be hidden in the heart of a distant mountain. The Eternal Flame was no ordinary fire; it was the very essence of life itself, a flame that burned with the purest energy, capable of granting unimaginable power to those who could harness it.

The legend of the Eternal Flame was ancient, passed down through the generations of the Phoenix Kingdom. It was said that the Eternal Flame was a gift from the gods, a source of divine power that had once been accessible to the Phoenix Kings of old. But over time, the location of the Eternal Flame had been lost, its secrets hidden away in a distant and dangerous land. The few who had attempted to find it had never returned, their fates unknown, swallowed by the perilous journey that awaited them.

The Phoenix King knew that if he were to truly fulfill his destiny, to protect the balance of Eldoria and ensure the continued prosperity of his people, he would need to find the Eternal Flame. The power it held could strengthen his connection to the fire, enhance his abilities, and give him the means to face the challenges that lay ahead. But the journey to find the Eternal Flame would be dangerous, fraught with unknown perils, and he would need to be prepared for whatever challenges awaited him.

As the Phoenix King meditated on the visions he had seen, he felt a sense of resolve growing within him. He knew that the time had come to embark on the next chapter of his journey, to seek out the Eternal Flame and unlock the power that it held. But he also knew that he could not undertake this journey alone—he would need the guidance and support of a trusted companion, someone who could help him navigate the dangers that lay ahead.

And so, the Phoenix King called upon Ignis, an ember sprite who had been his loyal companion since his childhood. Ignis was a small, fiery creature, with a body made entirely of glowing embers and a mischievous smile that belied his fierce loyalty. Though small in size, Ignis possessed a deep knowledge of the fire, and his ability to manipulate the flames made him an invaluable ally.

When Ignis arrived, the Phoenix King shared with him the visions he had seen and the journey that lay ahead. "I have seen the Eternal Flame, Ignis," the Phoenix King said, his voice filled with determination. "It is hidden in the heart of a distant mountain, a source of unlimited power that could help us protect the balance of our world. But the journey to find it will be dangerous, and I will need your help."

Ignis listened intently, his ember eyes glowing with curiosity and excitement. "The Eternal Flame... I've heard stories about it, but I never thought anyone would actually try to find it," he said, his voice crackling like the fire he was made of. "But if anyone can do it, it's you, my king. I'll go with you, wherever this journey takes us. We'll find the Eternal Flame together."

The Phoenix King smiled, grateful for Ignis' unwavering loyalty. "Thank you, Ignis," he replied, his heart swelling with determination. "Together, we will find the Eternal Flame, and we will bring its power back to our kingdom. The journey will be long and perilous, but I know that with your help, we can succeed."

And so, with Ignis by his side, the Phoenix King began to prepare for the journey ahead. He gathered supplies, consulted the elders of the Phoenix Kingdom for advice, and studied the maps and ancient texts that spoke of the distant mountain where the Eternal Flame was said to be hidden. The journey would take them across the Fire Plains, a vast and treacherous expanse of land where the ground was scorched and the air was thick with heat. It was a place where few dared to venture, for it was home to many dangers, including a tribe of fire giants who were said to guard the entrance to the mountain.

Despite the dangers, the Phoenix King knew that he had no choice but to press forward. The Eternal Flame was too important, too powerful to be left undiscovered. With Ignis by his side and the knowledge he had gained from the ancient texts, the Phoenix King felt confident that they could overcome whatever challenges lay ahead.

The Journey Begins

The day of departure arrived, and the Phoenix King stood at the edge of the Fire Plains, the vast expanse of scorched earth stretching out before him as far as the eye could see. The ground was cracked and dry, with steam rising from the fissures, and the air was filled with the acrid scent of sulfur. In the distance, the peaks of the distant mountains loomed, their tops shrouded in smoke and ash.

Ignis floated beside the Phoenix King, his ember eyes glowing with a mixture of excitement and caution. "This is it," he said, his voice crackling with energy. "The Fire Plains. I've heard stories about this place, about the fire giants that live here and the dangers that lurk beneath the surface. But we've come too far to turn back now. Are you ready?"

The Phoenix King nodded, his gaze fixed on the distant mountains. "I'm ready," he replied, his voice steady. "We must find the Eternal Flame, no matter the cost. The balance of our world depends on it."

With that, the Phoenix King and Ignis set out across the Fire Plains, the heat of the land rising around them as they made their way toward the distant mountains. The journey was difficult, the ground hot beneath their feet and the air thick with heat, but the Phoenix King was undeterred. He knew that the Eternal Flame was within his reach, and he was determined to find it.

As they traveled, Ignis used his knowledge of the fire to guide them, helping the Phoenix King navigate the treacherous landscape. The ground was unstable, with fissures opening and closing at random, and the air was filled with bursts of flame that erupted from the earth. But Ignis was quick and nimble, darting ahead to scout the path and warning the Phoenix King of any dangers that lay ahead.

The days turned into weeks as they crossed the Fire Plains, the journey long and arduous. The Phoenix King felt the weight of the journey bearing down on him, the heat sapping his strength and the constant vigilance required to navigate the landscape taking its toll. But he pressed on, driven by the knowledge that the Eternal Flame awaited him, that its power could help him protect the balance of the world.

One evening, as they camped beneath the stars, Ignis floated beside the Phoenix King, his ember body glowing softly in the darkness. "We've come a long way, haven't we?" he said, his voice filled with a mixture of exhaustion and pride. "I can see the mountains getting closer every day. We're almost there."

The Phoenix King nodded, his gaze fixed on the distant peaks. "Yes, we are," he replied, his voice steady. "But we must be cautious. The fire giants are said to guard the entrance to the mountain, and they will not let us pass easily. We must be prepared for whatever challenges they throw our way."

Ignis nodded, his ember eyes glowing with determination. "I'm with you, my king," he said, his voice crackling with resolve. "Whatever challenges lie ahead, we'll face them together."

The Phoenix King smiled, grateful for Ignis' unwavering loyalty. "Thank you, Ignis," he said, his voice filled with warmth. "Together, we will find the Eternal Flame and unlock its power. The journey may be difficult, but I know that we can succeed."

And so, with renewed determination, the Phoenix King and Ignis continued their journey across the Fire Plains, their eyes fixed on the distant mountains where the Eternal Flame awaited them.

The Fire Giants' Challenge

After many weeks of travel, the Phoenix King and Ignis finally reached the base of the distant mountains. The air was thick with heat and smoke, and the ground beneath their feet was blackened and cracked, as if the very earth had been scorched by the flames of the Eternal Flame. The mountains loomed above them, their peaks shrouded in ash and smoke, and the Phoenix King could feel the power of the Eternal Flame calling to him, urging him forward.

But as they approached the entrance to the mountain, a massive figure stepped out from the shadows, blocking their path. The figure was a fire giant, a towering creature made entirely of flame and molten rock, its eyes glowing with an intense, fiery light. The fire giant stood at least twice the height of the

Phoenix King, its massive body radiating heat that scorched the earth around it.

The Phoenix King and Ignis stopped in their tracks, their eyes fixed on the fire giant as it loomed over them. The giant's voice rumbled like an earthquake as it spoke, its words filled with power and authority. "Who dares to approach the Mountain of Flame?" the giant demanded, its voice echoing through the air. "This is sacred ground, guarded by the fire giants for centuries. No one may pass without proving their worth."

The Phoenix King stepped forward, his gaze steady as he faced the fire giant. "I am the Phoenix King, ruler of the Phoenix Kingdom," he said, his voice filled with determination. "I seek the Eternal Flame, a source of power that can help me protect the balance of our world. I ask for passage through the Mountain of Flame."

The fire giant regarded the Phoenix King with a piercing gaze, its fiery eyes glowing with intensity. "The Eternal Flame is not meant for the weak or the unworthy," the giant rumbled, its voice filled with warning. "Only those who can prove their strength and resolve may pass. If you wish to continue, you must face the trials of the fire giants. Only then will you be allowed to enter the mountain."

Ignis floated beside the Phoenix King, his ember eyes glowing with concern. "The trials of the fire giants are legendary," he whispered, his voice crackling with caution. "They're said to be impossible to complete, even for the strongest of warriors. Are you sure we can do this?"

The Phoenix King nodded, his gaze fixed on the fire giant. "We have no choice," he replied, his voice steady. "The Eternal Flame is too important. We must face the trials and prove ourselves worthy. Only then can we continue our journey."

The fire giant nodded, its massive form looming over them as it spoke. "Very well," the giant rumbled, its voice filled with authority. "You shall face the trials of the fire giants. But be warned—the trials are not for the faint of heart. They will test your strength, your resolve, and your understanding of the fire. If you fail, you will be consumed by the flames. If you succeed, you will be granted passage through the Mountain of Flame."

The Phoenix King took a deep breath, steeling himself for the trials ahead. He knew that the fire giants were powerful beings, ancient guardians of the

Eternal Flame, and that their trials would be unlike anything he had faced before. But he also knew that he had come too far to turn back now. The power of the Eternal Flame awaited him, and he was determined to prove himself worthy.

The First Trial: The Path of Fire

The fire giant led the Phoenix King and Ignis to the entrance of the mountain, where a narrow path wound its way up the steep slopes. The path was treacherous, with jagged rocks jutting out from the sides and rivers of molten lava flowing across the ground. The air was thick with heat and smoke, and the ground beneath their feet was unstable, shifting and cracking with every step.

"This is the Path of Fire," the fire giant rumbled, its voice echoing through the air. "It is the first of the trials. You must navigate the path without falling into the flames, without being consumed by the fire. Only those who can control the fire within themselves will succeed. If you fall, you will be lost forever."

The Phoenix King nodded, his gaze fixed on the narrow path ahead. He could feel the heat rising from the lava, the intensity of the flames pressing in on him, but he was determined to succeed. He knew that the Path of Fire would test his control over the flames, his ability to navigate the dangers that lay ahead.

Ignis floated beside him, his ember eyes glowing with concern. "Be careful, my king," he whispered, his voice crackling with worry. "The path is dangerous, and the flames are unforgiving. But I believe in you. I know you can do this."

The Phoenix King smiled, grateful for Ignis' support. "Thank you, Ignis," he replied, his voice filled with determination. "I will be careful. Together, we will navigate the Path of Fire and prove ourselves worthy."

With that, the Phoenix King took his first step onto the Path of Fire, the heat of the flames pressing in on him as he carefully navigated the narrow path. The ground beneath his feet was hot and unstable, shifting and cracking with every step, but the Phoenix King remained focused, his eyes fixed on the path ahead.

The flames rose up around him, their intensity growing with every step. The heat was overwhelming, the air thick with smoke, but the Phoenix King pressed on, his heart filled with resolve. He could feel the fire within him, the Immortal Fire that connected him to the Sacred Flame, giving him the strength and the control he needed to navigate the path.

As he made his way up the path, the Phoenix King encountered several obstacles—rivers of molten lava that flowed across the ground, jagged rocks that jutted out from the sides, and bursts of flame that erupted from the earth. But with Ignis' guidance and his own control over the fire, the Phoenix King was able to navigate each obstacle, moving steadily up the path.

The journey was long and arduous, the heat and the flames taking their toll on the Phoenix King. But he pressed on, driven by the knowledge that the Eternal Flame awaited him at the end of the trials. He knew that he had to prove himself worthy, that he had to demonstrate his control over the fire, his understanding of its dual nature.

Finally, after what felt like an eternity, the Phoenix King reached the top of the path, the flames receding as he stepped onto solid ground. He took a deep breath, his heart pounding with a mixture of exhaustion and relief. He had completed the first trial, had navigated the Path of Fire and proven his control over the flames.

Ignis floated beside him, his ember eyes glowing with pride. "You did it, my king," he said, his voice crackling with excitement. "You navigated the Path of Fire and proved yourself worthy. I knew you could do it."

The Phoenix King smiled, grateful for Ignis' support. "Thank you, Ignis," he replied, his voice filled with warmth. "But the trials are not over yet. We must continue, must face whatever challenges lie ahead."

The Second Trial: The Guardian of the Flame

As the Phoenix King and Ignis stood at the top of the Path of Fire, the fire giant reappeared, its massive form looming over them. "You have passed the first trial," the giant rumbled, its voice filled with authority. "But the trials are not yet complete. The second trial awaits you—the Guardian of the Flame."

The fire giant led them to a large, open chamber within the mountain, where a massive, glowing flame burned at the center. The flame was unlike any the Phoenix King had ever seen—it was pure and radiant, its light filling the chamber with a warm, golden glow. But as they approached the flame, the ground began to tremble, and a massive figure emerged from the shadows.

The Guardian of the Flame was a towering creature, its body made of molten rock and fire, its eyes glowing with an intense, fiery light. It was a being of immense power, a guardian that had protected the Eternal Flame for centuries. The Phoenix King could feel the heat radiating from the creature, the power that it held, and he knew that the second trial would be even more difficult than the first.

"The Guardian of the Flame will test your strength, your resolve, and your understanding of the fire," the fire giant rumbled, its voice filled with warning. "You must face the Guardian and prove yourself worthy. Only then will you be granted passage to the final trial."

The Phoenix King took a deep breath, steeling himself for the battle ahead. He knew that the Guardian of the Flame was a powerful being, a creature that had been created to protect the Eternal Flame, and that the battle would be a true test of his abilities.

Ignis floated beside him, his ember eyes glowing with concern. "The Guardian of the Flame is a powerful opponent," he whispered, his voice crackling with caution. "But I believe in you, my king. You've come this far, and I know you can succeed. Just remember what you've learned—control the fire within you, and you will prevail."

The Phoenix King nodded, his heart filled with determination. "Thank you, Ignis," he replied, his voice steady. "I will face the Guardian and prove myself worthy. The Eternal Flame awaits us, and I will not let anything stand in our way."

With that, the Phoenix King stepped forward, his gaze fixed on the Guardian of the Flame as it loomed before him. The creature's eyes glowed with intensity as it regarded the Phoenix King, its massive form radiating heat and power.

The Guardian of the Flame let out a roar, its voice echoing through the chamber as it charged toward the Phoenix King. The ground shook beneath its massive feet, the air filled with the sound of crackling flames as the creature unleashed its power.

The Phoenix King stood his ground, his heart filled with resolve as he prepared to face the Guardian. He could feel the fire within him, the Immortal

Fire that connected him to the Sacred Flame, giving him the strength and the power he needed to stand against the creature.

As the Guardian of the Flame approached, the Phoenix King summoned the fire within him, his wings glowing with a radiant light as he unleashed a burst of flames. The flames collided with the Guardian, the heat and light filling the chamber as the two forces clashed.

The battle was fierce, the flames raging as the Phoenix King and the Guardian of the Flame fought for control. The Phoenix King could feel the power of the Guardian, the intensity of its flames, but he refused to back down. He knew that he had the strength within him, that he had the power to control the fire and to overcome the creature.

The Guardian of the Flame roared, its massive form towering over the Phoenix King as it unleashed a torrent of fire. The heat was overwhelming, the flames searing the air around them, but the Phoenix King remained focused, his gaze fixed on the creature as he summoned the fire within him.

With a surge of power, the Phoenix King unleashed a powerful blast of flames, the intensity of the fire filling the chamber as it collided with the Guardian. The flames engulfed the creature, the heat and light overwhelming it as the Phoenix King poured all of his strength into the attack.

The Guardian of the Flame let out a final roar, its massive form trembling as the flames consumed it. The ground shook beneath their feet as the creature began to crumble, its body breaking apart as the fire within it was extinguished.

As the flames receded, the Phoenix King stood victorious, his heart filled with a mixture of exhaustion and relief. He had faced the Guardian of the Flame, had proven his strength and resolve, and had overcome the second trial.

Ignis floated beside him, his ember eyes glowing with pride. "You did it, my king," he said, his voice crackling with excitement. "You defeated the Guardian of the Flame and proved yourself worthy. I knew you could do it."

The Phoenix King smiled, grateful for Ignis' support. "Thank you, Ignis," he replied, his voice filled with warmth. "But the trials are not over yet. We must continue, must face the final challenge that awaits us."

The Final Trial: The Heart of the Mountain

With the second trial complete, the fire giant led the Phoenix King and Ignis to the heart of the mountain, where the Eternal Flame was said to be hidden. The air grew warmer as they descended deeper into the mountain, the walls glowing with a faint, golden light. The ground beneath their feet was solid and smooth, and the heat intensified with every step.

Finally, they reached a large chamber at the center of the mountain, where the air was thick with heat and the walls glowed with the light of the fire. At the center of the chamber, a massive, glowing flame burned, its light filling the room with a warm, golden glow. The Phoenix King could feel the power of the flame, the intensity of its energy, and he knew that this was the Eternal Flame—the source of unlimited power that he had sought for so long.

But as they approached the Eternal Flame, the fire giant stepped forward, its massive form looming over them. "You have proven yourself worthy," the giant rumbled, its voice filled with authority. "But there is one final trial that you must face. The Eternal Flame is not meant for the faint of heart. It is a source of immense power, but it is also a force of great responsibility. To claim the Eternal Flame, you must prove that you understand the true nature of the fire—that you understand the balance between creation and destruction, life and death."

The Phoenix King nodded, his gaze fixed on the Eternal Flame. "I understand," he replied, his voice steady. "I have faced the trials of the fire giants, have proven my strength and resolve. But I know that the Eternal Flame is more than just a source of power—it is a force of balance, of life and death. I am ready to face the final trial and to claim the power of the Eternal Flame."

The fire giant nodded, its fiery eyes glowing with intensity. "Very well," the giant rumbled. "The final trial is a test of your understanding of the fire, of the balance that it represents. You must step into the Eternal Flame and allow it to consume you. If you truly understand the balance of the fire, if you are worthy of its power, you will emerge unscathed. But if you are not, the flames will consume you, and you will be lost forever."

Ignis floated beside the Phoenix King, his ember eyes glowing with concern. "This is it, my king," he whispered, his voice crackling with worry. "The final trial. But I believe in you. I know you can do this. Just remember what you've learned—embrace the fire within you, and you will succeed."

The Phoenix King smiled, grateful for Ignis' support. "Thank you, Ignis," he replied, his voice filled with warmth. "I will remember what I've learned. I will embrace the fire, and I will prove myself worthy."

With that, the Phoenix King stepped forward, his heart filled with resolve as he approached the Eternal Flame. He could feel the heat of the flame, the intensity of its power, but he was undeterred. He knew that this was the final test, the ultimate challenge of his journey, and he was determined to succeed.

As he stepped into the Eternal Flame, the world around him seemed to dissolve into an inferno of light and heat. The flames engulfed him, their intensity overwhelming, but instead of pain, he felt a strange sense of clarity. The fire was not merely consuming him—it was transforming him, stripping away the layers of his being, revealing the essence of his soul.

The Phoenix King could feel the fire testing him, pushing him to his limits, but he remained focused, his heart filled with resolve. He knew that the Eternal Flame was more than just a source of power—it was a force of balance, of life and death, and he was determined to prove himself worthy.

As the flames intensified, the Phoenix King felt a surge of power unlike anything he had ever experienced. The fire within him, the Immortal Fire that connected him to the Sacred Flame, flared to life, filling him with a sense of purpose and determination. He understood now that the fire was not just a force of destruction—it was a force of renewal, of rebirth. It was the fire that gave life, that brought light to the darkness, that allowed the world to continue its eternal cycle.

With this understanding, the Phoenix King embraced the flames, allowing the fire to wash over him, to consume him. He could feel the heat, the light, the power of the fire, but instead of pain, he felt a sense of peace, of clarity. The flames were not consuming him—they were transforming him, burning away the doubts and fears, leaving only the essence of his soul.

The flames began to recede, the light fading, the heat dissipating. The Phoenix King opened his eyes, his vision clearing, and he found himself standing once more before the Eternal Flame, the fire that had tested his very soul.

The fire giant stepped forward, its massive form looming over the Phoenix King as it regarded him with a piercing gaze. "You have proven yourself worthy," the giant rumbled, its voice filled with authority. "You have faced the final trial, have embraced the fire, and have emerged unscathed. The power of the Eternal Flame is now yours."

The Phoenix King bowed his head in respect, his heart filled with a mixture of accomplishment and purpose. "Thank you," he replied, his voice steady. "I will use the power of the Eternal Flame to protect the balance of our world, to ensure that the cycles of life and death, creation and destruction, continue in harmony."

The fire giant nodded, its fiery eyes glowing with approval. "The Eternal Flame is a source of immense power, but it is also a great responsibility," the giant rumbled. "You have proven that you understand the balance of the fire, that you are worthy of its power. Use it wisely, Phoenix King, and you will protect the balance of our world."

The Phoenix King nodded, his heart filled with resolve. He knew that the journey had been long and difficult, but he had succeeded. He had faced the trials of the fire giants, had proven his strength, his resolve, and his understanding of the fire. He had claimed the power of the Eternal Flame, and with it, he would protect the balance of Eldoria.

As the Phoenix King and Ignis prepared to leave the mountain, the fire giant stepped aside, allowing them passage. The Phoenix King could feel the power of the Eternal Flame within him, the intensity of its energy filling him with a sense of purpose and determination. He knew that the journey was not over, that there were still challenges ahead, but he was ready to face them. He had the power of the Eternal Flame, the strength of the fire within him, and the knowledge of the balance that he had learned on his journey.

With Ignis by his side, the Phoenix King left the mountain, his heart filled with resolve. The journey had been long and perilous, but he had succeeded. He had claimed the power of the Eternal Flame, and with it, he would protect the balance of Eldoria, ensuring that the cycles of life and death, creation and destruction, continued in harmony.

The legend of the Phoenix King had truly begun, and the world of Eldoria would never be the same again.

Chapter 5: The Inferno of Trials

The Challenge of the Fire Giants

The journey to the heart of the mountain had been long and arduous, but the Phoenix King was far from finished. The Eternal Flame, a source of immense power and the key to maintaining the balance in Eldoria, remained just out of reach. Before he could claim this power, however, he had to prove his worth to the ancient guardians of the flame—the fire giants. These formidable beings were tasked with protecting the secrets of the Eternal Flame, ensuring that only those who truly understood the balance between destruction and renewal could access its power.

The fire giant who had led the Phoenix King and Ignis through the mountain stood before them, his massive form looming over the pair. His eyes, glowing like twin suns, were filled with an ancient, unyielding determination. He was the gatekeeper to the Eternal Flame, and his word would determine whether the Phoenix King would be allowed to continue.

"You have shown great strength and resilience, Phoenix King," the giant rumbled, his voice echoing through the chamber. "But strength alone is not enough. The Eternal Flame is a source of creation and destruction, of life and death. To wield its power, you must understand the delicate balance it represents. You must prove that you are worthy, not just in body, but in mind and spirit as well."

The Phoenix King nodded, his gaze steady. "I understand," he replied. "I am ready to face whatever trials you set before me."

The giant's eyes narrowed, assessing the Phoenix King's resolve. "Very well," he said after a moment's consideration. "You shall face the Inferno of Trials. These tests will challenge your wisdom, your courage, and your understanding of the balance that the Eternal Flame represents. Should you succeed, the path to the Eternal Flame will be revealed to you. Should you fail..." He let the implication hang in the air, the unspoken consequences clear.

The Phoenix King took a deep breath, feeling the weight of the moment. The trials ahead would not be easy—of that he was certain. But he had come too far to turn back now. The balance of Eldoria depended on him, and he was determined to prove himself worthy.

Ignis, the loyal ember sprite who had accompanied him on this journey, hovered at his side, his ember eyes glowing with a mixture of concern and determination. "We can do this," Ignis whispered, his voice crackling with resolve. "Whatever these trials throw at us, we'll face them together."

The Phoenix King smiled, grateful for Ignis's unwavering support. "Thank you, Ignis," he said softly. "Together, we will succeed."

With that, the fire giant raised his massive hand and gestured toward a doorway at the far end of the chamber. The door was made of solid obsidian, its surface etched with ancient runes that glowed faintly in the dim light. Beyond the door lay the Inferno of Trials—the first challenge the Phoenix King would face on his path to the Eternal Flame.

"You may begin," the giant said, stepping aside to allow the Phoenix King to pass. "Remember, these trials will test more than just your strength. They will challenge your mind, your spirit, and your understanding of the balance that you seek to protect."

The Phoenix King nodded once more, then turned to face the doorway. With a final deep breath, he stepped forward, crossing the threshold into the unknown, with Ignis close behind.

The Trial of Wisdom

The moment the Phoenix King stepped through the doorway, the temperature dropped sharply, and the oppressive heat of the mountain's core gave way to a chilling cold. He found himself standing in a vast cavern, its walls lined with jagged crystals that glowed with a pale, blue light. The air was thick with fog, obscuring his vision, and the ground beneath his feet was slick with ice.

This was the Trial of Wisdom, the first of the three trials he would face. It was a test not of physical strength, but of mental acuity and understanding. To pass this trial, the Phoenix King would need to demonstrate his ability to think critically, to solve problems, and to understand the deeper truths that lay beneath the surface.

As the Phoenix King took in his surroundings, a voice echoed through the cavern, deep and resonant. "Welcome, Phoenix King," the voice said. "This is the Trial of Wisdom. To proceed, you must solve the riddle that lies before you. Only then will the path forward be revealed."

The Phoenix King nodded, his mind already racing as he prepared for the challenge ahead. He knew that this trial would require more than just intelligence—it would require insight, intuition, and an understanding of the balance that governed all things.

The voice continued, the words reverberating through the cavern. "The riddle is this: I am both the beginning and the end, the light and the darkness, the creator and the destroyer. I am the force that drives the cycle of life, yet I am also the force that brings it to an end. What am I?"

The Phoenix King closed his eyes, focusing on the riddle. The answer seemed simple, almost too simple, but he knew that the trials of the fire giants were never straightforward. He needed to think deeply, to understand not just the surface meaning of the words, but the deeper truth they represented.

"I am both the beginning and the end," the Phoenix King repeated to himself, thinking aloud. "The light and the darkness, the creator and the destroyer. The force that drives the cycle of life, yet also brings it to an end..."

He opened his eyes, the answer clear in his mind. "Fire," he said confidently. "The answer is fire. Fire is the force that drives the cycle of life, providing warmth and light, yet it is also the force that brings destruction and death. It is the beginning and the end, the creator and the destroyer."

For a moment, there was only silence. Then, the voice spoke again, its tone filled with approval. "You have answered correctly, Phoenix King. Fire is indeed the answer. It is the force that governs all things, the balance between creation and destruction. You have shown wisdom in understanding this truth."

As the voice spoke, the fog in the cavern began to lift, revealing a path that led deeper into the mountain. The Phoenix King felt a surge of relief and pride, knowing that he had passed the first trial.

Ignis floated beside him, his ember eyes glowing with excitement. "You did it!" he exclaimed, his voice crackling with joy. "You solved the riddle! I knew you could do it!"

The Phoenix King smiled, grateful for Ignis's encouragement. "Thank you, Ignis," he said warmly. "But this is only the beginning. We still have two more trials to face."

With that, the Phoenix King and Ignis followed the newly revealed path, their steps echoing through the cavern as they moved forward to face the next challenge.

The Trial of Courage

The path from the Trial of Wisdom led the Phoenix King and Ignis to another chamber, this one filled with a searing heat that seemed to press down on them from all sides. The air was thick with the smell of sulfur, and the ground beneath their feet was hot to the touch. In the center of the chamber, a massive pit of molten lava bubbled and churned, casting an eerie, red glow over the walls.

This was the Trial of Courage, the second of the three trials the Phoenix King would face. It was a test of bravery and resolve, a challenge that would force him to confront his deepest fears and push beyond the limits of his endurance. To pass this trial, the Phoenix King would need to demonstrate not just physical bravery, but also the courage to face the unknown and the willingness to take risks for the greater good.

As the Phoenix King approached the pit of lava, the voice of the fire giants echoed through the chamber once more. "Welcome, Phoenix King," the voice said. "This is the Trial of Courage. To proceed, you must cross the pit of lava and reach the other side. But be warned—the path is treacherous, and the heat will test your resolve. Only those with true courage can succeed."

The Phoenix King looked down at the bubbling lava, feeling the intense heat radiating from the pit. The path across was narrow, little more than a series of precarious stones that jutted out from the molten surface. One wrong step, and he would be consumed by the flames.

Ignis floated beside him, his ember eyes glowing with concern. "This is going to be tough," he said, his voice crackling with worry. "But I know you can do it. Just stay focused, take it one step at a time, and you'll make it across."

The Phoenix King nodded, his heart pounding with a mixture of fear and determination. He knew that the Trial of Courage was designed to test his resolve, to push him to the brink of his endurance. But he also knew that he could not afford to fail. The balance of Eldoria depended on him, and he was determined to prove himself worthy.

With a deep breath, the Phoenix King stepped onto the first stone, feeling the heat of the lava beneath his feet. The stone was hot, almost unbearably so, but he forced himself to stay calm, to focus on the path ahead. One step at a time, he told himself. Just take it one step at a time.

He moved cautiously, carefully placing each foot on the next stone, his eyes fixed on the far side of the pit. The heat was intense, the air thick with the smell of burning rock, but the Phoenix King pressed on, his heart filled with resolve.

As he neared the center of the pit, the path became even more precarious, the stones smaller and more unstable. The Phoenix King could feel

the heat searing his feathers, the sweat pouring down his face, but he refused to give up. He knew that he had to keep moving, to stay focused on his goal.

But just as he was about to step onto the next stone, the ground beneath him shifted, causing him to lose his balance. He stumbled, his foot slipping dangerously close to the edge of the stone, the molten lava bubbling just inches below.

For a moment, the Phoenix King felt a surge of panic, his heart racing as he struggled to regain his balance. But then he remembered the lessons he had learned—the importance of staying calm in the face of danger, the need to trust in himself and in the fire within him.

Taking a deep breath, the Phoenix King steadied himself, his mind focused on the task at hand. He could feel the Immortal Fire within him, giving him the strength and the courage he needed to continue. With renewed determination, he took the next step, his foot landing firmly on the stone.

The rest of the journey across the pit was just as treacherous, but the Phoenix King remained focused, his heart filled with resolve. He could feel the heat of the lava, the intensity of the flames, but he refused to let fear control him. He knew that he had the courage within him to succeed.

Finally, after what felt like an eternity, the Phoenix King reached the other side of the pit, his heart pounding with a mixture of exhaustion and relief. He had passed the Trial of Courage, had faced his fears and proven his bravery.

Ignis floated beside him, his ember eyes glowing with pride. "You did it!" he exclaimed, his voice crackling with excitement. "You made it across the pit! I knew you could do it!"

The Phoenix King smiled, grateful for Ignis's support. "Thank you, Ignis," he said warmly. "But we still have one more trial to face. The hardest part is yet to come."

With that, the Phoenix King and Ignis continued on their journey, moving forward to face the final challenge of the Inferno of Trials.

The Trial of Balance

The path from the Trial of Courage led the Phoenix King and Ignis to the final chamber, a vast cavern filled with a radiant, golden light. The walls of the chamber were lined with glowing crystals, each one pulsating with a warm, soothing energy. In the center of the chamber, a massive, glowing flame burned, its light filling the room with a sense of peace and tranquility.

This was the Trial of Balance, the final and most difficult of the three trials. It was a test of the Phoenix King's understanding of the delicate balance between creation and destruction, life and death. To pass this trial, the Phoenix King would need to demonstrate not just his physical and mental abilities, but also his spiritual understanding of the fire and the balance it represented.

As the Phoenix King approached the glowing flame, the voice of the fire giants echoed through the chamber once more. "Welcome, Phoenix King," the voice said, its tone solemn and reverent. "This is the Trial of Balance. To proceed, you must demonstrate your understanding of the fire, of the balance between creation and destruction, life and death. The flame before you is a reflection of that balance—a source of both light and heat, of life and death. You must find the balance within yourself, and in doing so, you will find the key to unlocking the power of the Eternal Flame."

The Phoenix King nodded, his heart filled with a sense of purpose. He knew that this trial would be the most challenging, that it would require him to delve deep into his own soul and to confront the very essence of his being. But he was ready. He had faced the trials of wisdom and courage, had proven his strength and resolve, and now he was determined to prove his understanding of the balance that governed all things.

Ignis floated beside him, his ember eyes glowing with a mixture of awe and concern. "This is it, my king," he whispered, his voice crackling with reverence.

"The final trial. But I know you can do this. Just remember what you've learned—find the balance within yourself, and you'll succeed."

The Phoenix King smiled, grateful for Ignis's unwavering support. "Thank you, Ignis," he said softly. "I will find the balance. I will prove myself worthy."

With that, the Phoenix King stepped forward, his gaze fixed on the glowing flame. As he approached, he could feel the warmth of the fire, the light and heat radiating from its core. But he also sensed something deeper—an energy that pulsed beneath the surface, a force that connected the flame to the very fabric of existence.

Closing his eyes, the Phoenix King focused on the fire within him, the Immortal Fire that connected him to the Sacred Flame and to the balance that governed all things. He could feel the fire pulsing through his veins, could sense the dual nature of the flames—their power to create and to destroy, to give life and to take it away.

He understood now that the fire was not just a force of nature, but a reflection of the balance that existed within all things. It was the cycle of life and death, creation and destruction, that allowed the world to continue, that ensured the harmony of Eldoria.

As the Phoenix King meditated on this truth, the glowing flame before him began to shift, its light and heat intensifying. The ground beneath him trembled, and the air was filled with a deep, resonant hum. The Phoenix King could feel the power of the flame, the energy that it held, and he knew that the final test was about to begin.

The voice of the fire giants echoed through the chamber once more, its tone filled with a sense of gravity. "To pass the Trial of Balance, you must demonstrate your understanding of the fire, of the balance between creation and destruction, life and death. You must find the balance within yourself and use it to control the flame before you. Only then will you be granted the power of the Eternal Flame."

The Phoenix King nodded, his heart filled with resolve. He knew that this was the moment of truth, the ultimate test of his journey. Taking a deep breath, he focused on the fire within him, allowing its energy to fill him, to connect him to the flame before him.

With a steady hand, the Phoenix King reached out to the glowing flame, his fingers brushing against its surface. The moment his hand made contact, the flame flared to life, its light and heat surging with intensity. The Phoenix King could feel the power of the flame, the energy that it held, but he also sensed the danger—the potential for destruction if the balance was not maintained.

The Phoenix King focused on the balance within himself, on the understanding that he had gained throughout his journey. He could feel the fire pulsing through him, the dual nature of the flames—their power to create and to destroy, to give life and to take it away. He knew that he had to find the balance, to control the flame without letting it consume him.

Slowly, carefully, the Phoenix King began to channel the energy of the flame, using his understanding of the balance to guide it. He could feel the flame responding to his touch, its light and heat intensifying as he channeled its power. But he also knew that he had to be careful, that the flame was a powerful force that could easily spiral out of control if the balance was not maintained.

As the Phoenix King continued to channel the flame, the ground beneath him trembled, and the air was filled with a deep, resonant hum. The flame flared to life, its light and heat surging with intensity, but the Phoenix King remained focused, his heart filled with resolve. He could feel the balance within him, the understanding that he had gained throughout his journey, and he knew that he was in control.

Finally, after what felt like an eternity, the Phoenix King succeeded in channeling the flame, its energy flowing through him in a steady, controlled stream. The flame pulsed with light and heat, its energy filling the chamber, but the Phoenix King remained calm, his mind focused on the balance that he had achieved.

As the flame settled, the ground beneath him stopped trembling, and the deep, resonant hum faded into silence. The Phoenix King opened his eyes, his gaze fixed on the glowing flame before him. He had passed the Trial of Balance, had demonstrated his understanding of the fire and the balance that it represented.

The voice of the fire giants echoed through the chamber once more, its tone filled with approval. "You have passed the Trial of Balance, Phoenix King," the voice said. "You have demonstrated your understanding of the fire, of the balance between creation and destruction, life and death. You are now worthy of the power of the Eternal Flame."

The Phoenix King bowed his head in respect, his heart filled with a mixture of accomplishment and purpose. "Thank you," he replied, his voice steady. "I will use the power of the Eternal Flame to protect the balance of our world, to ensure that the cycles of life and death, creation and destruction, continue in harmony."

With the final trial complete, the glowing flame before the Phoenix King began to shift, its light intensifying as it revealed the path to the Eternal Flame. The walls of the chamber glowed with a warm, golden light, and the air was filled with a sense of peace and tranquility.

Ignis floated beside the Phoenix King, his ember eyes glowing with pride. "You did it, my king!" he exclaimed, his voice crackling with excitement. "You passed the Trial of Balance! I knew you could do it!"

The Phoenix King smiled, grateful for Ignis's unwavering support. "Thank you, Ignis," he said softly. "Together, we have completed the Inferno of Trials. The path to the Eternal Flame is now open, and we can finally claim its power."

With that, the Phoenix King and Ignis followed the newly revealed path, their steps echoing through the chamber as they moved forward to claim the power of the Eternal Flame.

The Revelation of the Eternal Flame

As the Phoenix King and Ignis followed the path revealed by the glowing flame, the air grew warmer, and the golden light that filled the chamber intensified. The walls of the chamber were lined with glowing crystals, each one pulsating with a warm, soothing energy. The path led them deeper into the heart of the mountain, toward the source of the Eternal Flame.

Finally, after what felt like an eternity, the Phoenix King and Ignis reached the end of the path, where a massive, glowing chamber awaited them. The chamber was filled with a radiant, golden light, its walls lined with crystals that pulsed with energy. In the center of the chamber, a massive, glowing flame burned, its light filling the room with a sense of peace and tranquility.

The Phoenix King could feel the power of the Eternal Flame, the intensity of its energy filling the chamber. The flame was pure and radiant, its light and heat pulsing with life. The Phoenix King knew that this was the source of the power that he had sought for so long, the key to maintaining the balance of Eldoria.

As the Phoenix King approached the Eternal Flame, the voice of the fire giants echoed through the chamber once more, its tone filled with reverence. "Welcome, Phoenix King," the voice said. "You have passed the Inferno of Trials, have proven your strength, your resolve, and your understanding of the balance that governs all things. You are now worthy of the power of the Eternal Flame."

The Phoenix King nodded, his heart filled with a sense of purpose. He knew that the journey had been long and difficult, but he had succeeded. He had faced the trials of the fire giants, had proven his strength, his resolve, and his understanding of the fire. He had claimed the power of the Eternal Flame, and with it, he would protect the balance of Eldoria.

With a steady hand, the Phoenix King reached out to the Eternal Flame, his fingers brushing against its surface. The moment his hand made contact, the flame flared to life, its light and heat surging with intensity. The Phoenix King could feel the power of the flame, the energy that it held, and he knew that he had finally achieved his goal.

As the Phoenix King channeled the energy of the Eternal Flame, the ground beneath him trembled, and the air was filled with a deep, resonant hum. The flame pulsed with light and heat, its energy flowing through him in a steady, controlled stream. The Phoenix King could feel the balance within him, the understanding that he had gained throughout his journey, and he knew that he was in control.

Finally, after what felt like an eternity, the Phoenix King succeeded in channeling the power of the Eternal Flame, its energy flowing through him in a steady, controlled stream. The flame pulsed with light and heat, its energy filling the chamber, but the Phoenix King remained calm, his mind focused on the balance that he had achieved.

As the flame settled, the ground beneath him stopped trembling, and the deep, resonant hum faded into silence. The Phoenix King opened his eyes, his gaze fixed on the glowing flame before him. He had claimed the power of the Eternal Flame, had proven himself worthy, and with it, he would protect the balance of Eldoria.

Ignis floated beside him, his ember eyes glowing with pride. "You did it, my king!" he exclaimed, his voice crackling with excitement. "You claimed the power of the Eternal Flame! I knew you could do it!"

The Phoenix King smiled, grateful for Ignis's unwavering support. "Thank you, Ignis," he said softly. "Together, we have completed the Inferno of Trials. We have claimed the power of the Eternal Flame, and with it, we will protect the balance of our world."

With the power of the Eternal Flame now in his possession, the Phoenix King knew that his journey was far from over. There were still challenges ahead, still battles to be fought, but he was ready. He had the strength, the resolve, and the understanding to protect the balance of Eldoria, to ensure that the cycles of life and death, creation and destruction, continued in harmony.

As the Phoenix King and Ignis left the chamber, their hearts filled with resolve, they knew that the legend of the Phoenix King had truly begun, and that the world of Eldoria would never be the same again.

Chapter 6: The Heart of the Mountain

The Approach to the Mountain

The journey to the mountain where the Eternal Flame was said to reside had been long and fraught with peril, but the Phoenix King and his loyal companion, Ignis, had finally arrived. The mountain loomed before them, its peak shrouded in swirling clouds of ash and smoke. The air was thick with the scent of sulfur, and the ground beneath their feet was hot to the touch, as if the very earth itself was alive with the fire that burned within the mountain's core.

This was no ordinary mountain; it was a place of ancient power, a place where the elements of fire and earth converged in a dance of creation and destruction. The Phoenix King could feel the energy of the mountain pulsing through the ground, resonating with the fire within him. He knew that this was the place where the Eternal Flame awaited, a source of unlimited power that could help him protect the balance of Eldoria. But he also knew that the path ahead would not be easy. The mountain was guarded by powerful beings, ancient fire dragons who had watched over the Eternal Flame for centuries. These dragons were not merely creatures of myth and legend—they were embodiments of the elemental forces, beings of immense power and wisdom. To claim the Eternal Flame, the Phoenix King would need to prove his purity of heart, his worthiness, and his understanding of the balance that the flame represented.

Ignis, the ember sprite who had accompanied the Phoenix King on his journey, floated beside him, his ember eyes glowing with a mixture of awe and concern. "This is it," Ignis whispered, his voice crackling with anticipation. "The mountain where the Eternal Flame resides. But be careful, my king. The fire dragons are ancient and powerful. They will not let us pass easily."

The Phoenix King nodded, his gaze fixed on the mountain's peak. "I understand, Ignis," he replied, his voice steady. "But we have come too far to turn back now. The Eternal Flame is too important, too powerful to be left undiscovered. We must face whatever challenges lie ahead and prove ourselves worthy."

With that, the Phoenix King and Ignis began their ascent, climbing the steep, rocky slopes of the mountain. The path was treacherous, with jagged rocks jutting out from the sides and rivers of molten lava flowing across the ground. The air grew hotter with each step, and the ground beneath their feet trembled with the energy of the fire that burned within the mountain's core.

As they climbed higher, the Phoenix King could feel the presence of the fire dragons growing stronger, their ancient power resonating through the air. He knew that they were being watched, that the dragons were aware of their presence and were waiting for the right moment to reveal themselves.

Finally, after hours of arduous climbing, the Phoenix King and Ignis reached the entrance to the mountain's core—a massive, cavernous opening that led deep into the heart of the mountain. The entrance was guarded by two towering statues, each one carved in the likeness of a dragon, their eyes glowing with an inner fire. The air was thick with the scent of sulfur, and the ground beneath their feet was hot and unstable, shifting and cracking with the energy of the fire that burned within.

"This is it," Ignis whispered, his voice filled with awe. "The entrance to the heart of the mountain, where the Eternal Flame resides. But be careful, my king. The fire dragons will be waiting for us inside."

The Phoenix King nodded, his heart pounding with a mixture of anticipation and resolve. He knew that the final challenge awaited him within the mountain's core, that he would need to confront the fire dragons and prove his worthiness to claim the Eternal Flame.

Taking a deep breath, the Phoenix King stepped forward, crossing the threshold into the heart of the mountain.

The Encounter with the Fire Dragons

The moment the Phoenix King and Ignis entered the heart of the mountain, they were met with an overwhelming wave of heat and light. The cavern was vast, its walls lined with glowing crystals that pulsed with the energy of the fire that burned within the mountain's core. Rivers of molten lava flowed through the chamber, casting an eerie, red glow over the walls. The air was thick with the scent of sulfur, and the ground beneath their feet trembled with the power of the fire that raged below.

But it was not the heat or the light that drew the Phoenix King's attention—it was the presence of the fire dragons. These ancient beings, who had guarded the Eternal Flame for centuries, were unlike anything the Phoenix King had ever seen. They were massive, towering creatures, their bodies made entirely of fire and molten rock. Their eyes burned with an intense, fiery light, and their wings, made of pure flame, cast a radiant glow over the cavern.

There were three fire dragons, each one larger and more imposing than the last. The first dragon, with scales the color of molten lava, stood at the far end of the chamber, its eyes fixed on the Phoenix King. The second dragon, with wings made of blue flame, hovered above the lava river, its gaze filled with a mixture of curiosity and caution. The third dragon, the largest and most powerful of the three, stood at the center of the chamber, its eyes glowing with a deep, ancient wisdom.

As the Phoenix King and Ignis approached, the third dragon stepped forward, its massive form towering over them. The dragon's voice rumbled like an earthquake, deep and resonant, as it addressed the Phoenix King. "Who dares to enter the heart of the mountain?" the dragon demanded, its voice filled with authority. "Who dares to seek the power of the Eternal Flame?"

The Phoenix King stepped forward, his gaze steady as he faced the dragon. "I am the Phoenix King, ruler of the Phoenix Kingdom," he replied, his voice filled with determination. "I seek the Eternal Flame, a source of power that can help me protect the balance of our world. I have come to prove my worthiness to claim its power."

The dragon regarded the Phoenix King with a piercing gaze, its fiery eyes seeming to see into the very depths of his soul. "The Eternal Flame is a source of immense power," the dragon rumbled, its voice filled with warning. "But it is also a force of great responsibility. To claim its power, you must prove that you are worthy—not just in strength, but in purity of heart. You must confront your deepest fears and insecurities, and you must demonstrate your understanding of the balance between destruction and renewal. Only then will you be granted the power of the Eternal Flame."

The Phoenix King nodded, his heart filled with resolve. "I understand," he replied, his voice steady. "I am ready to face whatever challenges lie ahead and to prove my worthiness to claim the power of the Eternal Flame."

The dragon's eyes narrowed, assessing the Phoenix King's resolve. "Very well," the dragon rumbled after a moment's consideration. "You shall face the Trial of the Heart. This trial will challenge your spirit, your courage, and your understanding of the fire that burns within you. You will be forced to confront your deepest fears and insecurities, and you will need to demonstrate that you are pure of heart. Only then will you be deemed worthy of the Eternal Flame."

The Phoenix King took a deep breath, steeling himself for the trial ahead. He knew that this would be the most difficult challenge he had ever faced, that it would require him to delve deep into his own soul and to confront the very essence of his being. But he was ready. He had come too far to turn back now, and he was determined to prove himself worthy of the Eternal Flame.

With that, the fire dragons stepped aside, revealing a glowing, fiery portal at the far end of the chamber. The portal pulsed with energy, its surface shimmering like liquid fire. The Phoenix King knew that this portal would lead him to the Trial of the Heart, to the final test that awaited him within the heart of the mountain.

Ignis floated beside him, his ember eyes glowing with concern. "This is it, my king," he whispered, his voice crackling with worry. "The final trial. But I believe in you. I know you can do this. Just remember what you've learned—find the balance within yourself, and you'll succeed."

The Phoenix King smiled, grateful for Ignis's unwavering support. "Thank you, Ignis," he said softly. "I will find the balance. I will prove myself worthy."

With that, the Phoenix King stepped forward, crossing the threshold into the portal and entering the Trial of the Heart.

The Trial of the Heart

The moment the Phoenix King stepped through the portal, he was enveloped in a blinding light, the heat of the flames intensifying as he was transported to a new realm. When the light faded, he found himself standing in a vast, empty void, the ground beneath his feet a smooth, obsidian surface that stretched out endlessly in all directions. The air was still and silent, the only sound the faint crackle of fire in the distance.

This was the Trial of the Heart, the final test that would determine whether the Phoenix King was truly worthy of the power of the Eternal Flame. Unlike the previous trials, this one was not a test of physical strength or mental acuity—it was a test of the spirit, a challenge that would force the Phoenix King to confront his deepest fears and insecurities, to prove that he was pure of heart.

As the Phoenix King stood in the void, the voice of the fire dragons echoed through the air, deep and resonant. "Welcome, Phoenix King," the voice said. "This is the Trial of the Heart. To pass this trial, you must confront your deepest fears and insecurities. You must prove that you are pure of heart, that you understand the balance between destruction and renewal, life and death. Only then will you be deemed worthy of the Eternal Flame."

The Phoenix King nodded, his heart filled with resolve. He knew that this trial would be the most difficult challenge he had ever faced, but he was ready. He had come too far to turn back now, and he was determined to prove himself worthy.

As the Phoenix King prepared for the trial, the void around him began to shift, the obsidian surface rippling like water. The air grew thick with tension, and the distant crackle of fire grew louder, filling the void with a sense of impending danger.

Suddenly, the ground beneath the Phoenix King's feet began to tremble, and the void around him was filled with a blinding light. When the light faded, the Phoenix King found himself standing in a familiar place—a place that he had not seen in many years, but that still haunted his dreams.

It was the Sacred Flame, the place of his birth, the heart of the Phoenix Kingdom. The flames burned bright and fierce, their light casting long shadows across the ground. The Phoenix King could feel the heat of the flames, the intensity of the fire that had given him life. But there was something wrong—something that sent a chill down his spine.

The flames were burning out of control, their light and heat growing more intense by the second. The ground beneath the Phoenix King's feet was cracking, the very earth trembling with the force of the fire. The air was thick with smoke, and the distant sound of crackling flames grew louder, filling the air with a sense of impending doom.

As the Phoenix King looked around, he saw the faces of the Fireborn, his people, their eyes filled with fear and desperation. They were trapped, surrounded by the flames, unable to escape the inferno that was consuming their world.

The Phoenix King's heart pounded with fear and guilt, his mind racing with a thousand thoughts. This was his greatest fear—the fear that he would not be able to protect his people, that he would fail in his duty as their king. The fire that had given him life, that had made him who he was, was now threatening to consume everything he held dear.

As the flames grew more intense, the Phoenix King felt his resolve begin to waver. The heat was overwhelming, the fear in his heart growing stronger with each passing moment. But then he remembered the lessons he had learned—the importance of balance, of understanding the dual nature of the fire. He knew that the fire was not just a force of destruction—it was also a force of creation, of renewal.

Taking a deep breath, the Phoenix King focused on the fire within him, the Immortal Fire that connected him to the Sacred Flame. He could feel the fire pulsing through his veins, giving him the strength and the courage he needed to face his fears. He knew that he had to remain calm, to find the balance within himself.

With renewed determination, the Phoenix King stepped forward, his gaze fixed on the flames. He could feel the heat, the intensity of the fire, but he refused to let fear control him. He knew that he had the power within him to control the flames, to bring balance to the fire that raged around him.

Slowly, carefully, the Phoenix King began to channel the energy of the fire, using his understanding of the balance to guide it. He could feel the flames responding to his touch, their intensity decreasing as he channeled their power. The fire that had once threatened to consume everything was now under his control, its energy flowing through him in a steady, controlled stream.

As the flames settled, the ground beneath the Phoenix King's feet stopped trembling, and the air was filled with a sense of peace and tranquility. The faces of the Fireborn, once filled with fear, were now filled with relief and gratitude. The Phoenix King had succeeded—he had confronted his deepest fear and had proven his ability to control the fire within him.

But the trial was not over yet. As the flames faded, the void around the Phoenix King shifted once more, the obsidian surface rippling like water. The air grew thick with tension, and the distant crackle of fire grew louder, filling the void with a sense of impending danger.

Suddenly, the ground beneath the Phoenix King's feet began to tremble once more, and the void around him was filled with a blinding light. When the light faded, the Phoenix King found himself standing in a new place—a place that he had never seen before, but that filled him with a sense of unease.

It was a barren wasteland, the ground cracked and dry, the sky dark and foreboding. The air was thick with the scent of ash, and the ground beneath the Phoenix King's feet was hot and unstable. The landscape was desolate, devoid of life, as if the very essence of the world had been drained away.

As the Phoenix King looked around, he saw the faces of the Fireborn, their eyes filled with despair and hopelessness. They were lost, wandering aimlessly through the wasteland, their once vibrant spirits now broken and defeated.

The Phoenix King's heart pounded with fear and guilt, his mind racing with a thousand thoughts. This was his greatest insecurity—the fear that he would not be able to bring renewal to his people, that he would fail in his duty to protect the balance of the world. The fire that had once given life and light was now a mere ember, threatening to extinguish forever.

As the Phoenix King stood in the wasteland, he felt his resolve begin to waver once more. The despair in his heart was overwhelming, the sense of hopelessness growing stronger with each passing moment. But then he remembered the lessons he had learned—the importance of renewal, of understanding the cycle of life and death. He knew that the fire was not just a force of creation—it was also a force of destruction, of rebirth.

Taking a deep breath, the Phoenix King focused on the fire within him, the Immortal Fire that connected him to the Sacred Flame. He could feel the fire pulsing through his veins, giving him the strength and the courage he needed to face his insecurities. He knew that he had to remain calm, to find the balance within himself.

With renewed determination, the Phoenix King stepped forward, his gaze fixed on the wasteland. He could feel the heat, the intensity of the fire, but he refused to let despair control him. He knew that he had the power within him to bring renewal to the world, to restore the balance that had been lost.

Slowly, carefully, the Phoenix King began to channel the energy of the fire, using his understanding of the balance to guide it. He could feel the flames within him growing stronger, their light and heat intensifying as he channeled their power. The fire that had once been a mere ember was now a blazing inferno, its energy filling the wasteland with life and light.

As the flames settled, the ground beneath the Phoenix King's feet stopped trembling, and the air was filled with a sense of peace and tranquility. The faces of the Fireborn, once filled with despair, were now filled with hope and joy. The Phoenix King had succeeded—he had confronted his deepest insecurity and had proven his ability to bring renewal to the world.

Proving His Worthiness

As the Phoenix King stood in the wasteland, the void around him began to shift once more, the obsidian surface rippling like water. The air grew thick with tension, and the distant crackle of fire grew louder, filling the void with a sense of impending danger.

But this time, the Phoenix King felt no fear or insecurity. He had faced his deepest fears and had proven his ability to control the fire within him. He had demonstrated his understanding of the balance between destruction and renewal, life and death. He knew that he was worthy of the power of the Eternal Flame.

The void around the Phoenix King was filled with a blinding light, the heat of the flames intensifying as he was transported back to the heart of the mountain. When the light faded, he found himself standing once more in the vast cavern, the walls lined with glowing crystals that pulsed with the energy of the fire that burned within the mountain's core. The fire dragons were waiting for him, their eyes filled with a deep, ancient wisdom.

The third dragon, the largest and most powerful of the three, stepped forward, its massive form towering over the Phoenix King. "You have passed the Trial of the Heart," the dragon rumbled, its voice filled with approval. "You have confronted your deepest fears and insecurities, and you have proven that you are pure of heart. You have demonstrated your understanding of the balance between destruction and renewal, life and death. You are now worthy of the power of the Eternal Flame."

The Phoenix King bowed his head in respect, his heart filled with a mixture of accomplishment and purpose. "Thank you," he replied, his voice steady. "I will use the power of the Eternal Flame to protect the balance of our world, to ensure that the cycles of life and death, creation and destruction, continue in harmony."

The dragon nodded, its fiery eyes glowing with approval. "The Eternal Flame is a source of immense power, but it is also a great responsibility," the dragon rumbled. "You have proven that you understand the balance of the fire, that you are worthy of its power. Use it wisely, Phoenix King, and you will protect the balance of our world."

With the final trial complete, the Phoenix King felt a surge of energy, the power of the Eternal Flame filling him with a sense of purpose and determination. He knew that his journey was far from over, that there were still challenges ahead, but he was ready to face them. He had the strength, the resolve, and the understanding to protect the balance of Eldoria, to ensure that the cycles of life and death, creation and destruction, continued in harmony.

As the Phoenix King and Ignis left the heart of the mountain, their hearts filled with resolve, they knew that the legend of the Phoenix King had truly begun, and that the world of Eldoria would never be the same again.

Chapter 7: The Flames of Rebirth

The Encounter with the Eternal Flame

After a journey that had tested his strength, wisdom, courage, and heart, the Phoenix King now stood at the threshold of his ultimate destiny. He had passed the trials of the fire giants, proved his worthiness to the ancient fire dragons, and confronted the deepest recesses of his soul. Now, only one task remained: to claim the power of the Eternal Flame.

The cavern where the Eternal Flame resided was unlike anything the Phoenix King had ever seen. The walls glistened with veins of molten rock, glowing with a radiant light that pulsed in time with the beat of the mountain's fiery heart. At the center of the chamber, surrounded by a ring of pure, glowing crystals, was the Eternal Flame—a pillar of fire that burned with an intensity unmatched by any flame in Eldoria.

The flame was alive, its tendrils dancing in a rhythm both mesmerizing and terrifying. It was a force of creation and destruction, of life and death, and the Phoenix King could feel its power radiating through the chamber, resonating with the fire that burned within his own soul.

Ignis, the loyal ember sprite who had accompanied the Phoenix King on his journey, floated beside him, his ember eyes wide with awe. "This is it," Ignis whispered, his voice crackling with reverence. "The Eternal Flame. I can feel its power, my king. It's incredible... and terrifying."

The Phoenix King nodded, his gaze fixed on the blazing pillar of fire before him. "It is a force unlike any other," he replied, his voice steady. "But it is also a force that must be understood, respected, and balanced. The fire can create and destroy, give life and take it away. To wield its power, one must understand the delicate balance between these forces."

Ignis floated closer to the Phoenix King, his voice filled with concern. "Are you ready for this, my king? Once you absorb the power of the Eternal Flame, there's no going back. You will be forever changed, your destiny intertwined with the flame."

The Phoenix King took a deep breath, his heart filled with a mixture of anticipation and resolve. "I am ready," he replied, his voice filled with determination. "I have come this far, faced every challenge that has been placed before me. I am ready to embrace the power of the Eternal Flame and to use it to protect the balance of our world."

With that, the Phoenix King stepped forward, his eyes fixed on the Eternal Flame. He could feel its heat intensifying as he approached, the energy within the chamber growing more powerful with each step. The flames seemed to call out to him, beckoning him to come closer, to embrace their power.

As the Phoenix King reached the edge of the ring of crystals that surrounded the Eternal Flame, he paused, his heart pounding with anticipation. He knew that this moment would define his destiny, that once he absorbed the power of the flame, he would be forever changed.

Taking a deep breath, the Phoenix King stepped into the ring, crossing the threshold that separated him from the Eternal Flame. The moment his foot touched the ground within the circle, the flames flared to life, their light and heat surging with an intensity that took his breath away.

The Phoenix King could feel the power of the flame, its energy pulsing through the air, resonating with the fire within him. He knew that the time had come to embrace the flame, to absorb its power and unlock his full potential.

With a steady hand, the Phoenix King reached out to the Eternal Flame, his fingers brushing against its surface. The moment his hand made contact, the flame flared even brighter, its light and heat enveloping him in a blinding inferno. The Phoenix King felt the fire surge through him, filling every part of his being with an overwhelming power.

The flames were not just burning him—they were transforming him, reshaping his very essence. The Phoenix King could feel the power of the flame coursing through his veins, merging with the fire that had always burned within him. It was a power unlike anything he had ever known, a force of pure creation and destruction, of life and death.

The transformation was both exhilarating and terrifying. The Phoenix King could feel himself becoming one with the flame, his body and soul intertwined with its energy. The fire was a part of him now, its power flowing through him like a river of molten lava.

As the flames continued to burn, the Phoenix King felt his consciousness expanding, his understanding of the fire deepening. He could see the intricate web of energy that connected all things, the cycle of life and death, creation and destruction that governed the world. He understood now that the fire was not just a tool or a weapon—it was the very essence of life itself, a force that must be wielded with care and wisdom.

Finally, after what felt like an eternity, the flames began to recede, their light and heat fading as they settled within the Phoenix King's body. The transformation was complete, and the Phoenix King stood before the Eternal Flame, his heart filled with a newfound sense of power and purpose.

He had absorbed the power of the Eternal Flame, had unlocked his full potential, and had become something more than he had ever imagined. The fire within him was stronger now, more powerful than ever before, and with it came a deeper understanding of the balance between life and death, creation and destruction.

Ignis floated beside him, his ember eyes glowing with awe. "My king... you did it," he whispered, his voice filled with reverence. "You absorbed the power of the Eternal Flame. You've unlocked your full potential. But... what does this mean?"

The Phoenix King looked down at his hands, feeling the energy of the flame pulsing through his veins. "It means that I have become something more," he replied, his voice steady. "I have become a symbol of hope and renewal, a force that can bring life where there was once only death. But it also means that I must bear the burden of this power, that I must ensure the balance between creation and destruction, life and death."

Ignis floated closer, his voice filled with concern. "But what does that burden entail? What must you do now?"

The Phoenix King took a deep breath, his heart heavy with the weight of his new responsibility. "I must protect the balance of our world," he replied, his voice filled with determination. "I must use this power to ensure that the cycles of life and death, creation and destruction, continue in harmony. I must be a guardian of the flame, a protector of the balance."

With that, the Phoenix King turned to face the Eternal Flame, his heart filled with resolve. He knew that his journey was far from over, that there were still challenges ahead, but he was ready to face them. He had the power of the Eternal Flame within him, and with it, he would protect the balance of Eldoria.

The Power of Resurrection

As the Phoenix King and Ignis made their way back through the mountain, the Phoenix King could feel the power of the Eternal Flame coursing through him, filling him with a sense of purpose and determination. The fire within him was stronger now, more powerful than ever before, and with it came a deeper understanding of his role as the guardian of the balance.

But as they descended from the mountain, the Phoenix King began to notice something strange. The fire within him seemed to resonate with the energy of the world around him, connecting him to the very essence of life itself. He could feel the pulse of the earth, the rhythm of the seasons, the cycle of life and death that governed all things.

It was then that the Phoenix King realized the true extent of the power he had gained. The Eternal Flame had given him more than just the ability to control the fire—it had given him the power of resurrection, the ability to bring life to those who had fallen, to restore what had been lost.

The realization was both exhilarating and terrifying. The Phoenix King knew that this power could be a force for great good, a way to heal the wounds of the world and to bring hope to those who had lost everything. But he also knew that it was a power that must be wielded with care and wisdom, that the balance between life and death must be maintained.

As they continued their descent, the Phoenix King and Ignis came across a small village at the base of the mountain. The village had been devastated by a recent volcanic eruption, its buildings reduced to rubble and its people left homeless and destitute. The air was thick with the scent of ash, and the ground beneath their feet was hot and unstable, shifting with the energy of the earth.

The villagers, seeing the Phoenix King approach, rushed to meet him, their eyes filled with desperation and hope. "Please, Phoenix King," one of the villagers cried, her voice trembling with emotion. "Our village has been destroyed, our homes reduced to ash. We have lost everything... our loved ones, our livelihoods... everything."

The Phoenix King's heart ached with empathy as he listened to the villagers' pleas. He could feel the pain and loss that they had endured, the weight of their suffering pressing down on them like a heavy burden. He knew that he had the power to help them, to restore what had been lost, but he also knew that he had to be careful, that the balance between life and death must be maintained.

Taking a deep breath, the Phoenix King stepped forward, his gaze steady as he addressed the villagers. "I understand your pain," he said, his voice filled with compassion. "I can feel the weight of your loss, the burden of your suffering. And I want to help you. But you must understand that the power of the Eternal Flame is a force of both creation and destruction, of life and death. To wield this power, I must ensure that the balance is maintained."

The villagers looked at the Phoenix King with a mixture of hope and fear, their eyes filled with uncertainty. "What do you mean, Phoenix King?" one of the villagers asked, her voice trembling. "What balance?"

The Phoenix King took another deep breath, his heart heavy with the weight of his new responsibility. "The balance between life and death is delicate," he replied, his voice steady. "The Eternal Flame is a force of creation, but it is also a force of destruction. To bring life where there was once only death, I must ensure that the balance is maintained. If I were to resurrect those who have fallen without consideration for the balance, I could disrupt the natural order of the world, causing more harm than good."

The villagers listened in silence, their faces filled with a mixture of understanding and fear. They knew that the Phoenix King was right, that the power of resurrection was not something to be taken lightly. But they also knew that they had nothing left to lose, that they were willing to do anything to restore what had been lost.

"We understand, Phoenix King," one of the villagers said, her voice filled with resolve. "We trust you to do what is right. Please, help us. We are willing to accept the consequences, whatever they may be."

The Phoenix King nodded, his heart filled with a sense of purpose. He knew that this was a moment of truth, that he had to make a decision that would define his role as the guardian of the balance. Taking a deep breath, he stepped forward, his gaze fixed on the villagers.

"Very well," the Phoenix King said, his voice steady. "I will help you. But you must understand that the power of the Eternal Flame is not something to be taken lightly. I will restore what has been lost, but I will do so in a way that ensures the balance is maintained."

With that, the Phoenix King closed his eyes, focusing on the fire within him, the Immortal Fire that connected him to the Eternal Flame. He could feel the power of the flame surging through him, resonating with the energy of the world around him. The fire was a force of creation and destruction, of life and death, and the Phoenix King knew that he had to wield it with care and wisdom.

Slowly, carefully, the Phoenix King began to channel the energy of the flame, using his understanding of the balance to guide it. He could feel the fire responding to his touch, its light and heat intensifying as he channeled its power. The energy of the flame flowed through him, filling the air with a radiant light that seemed to pulse in time with the rhythm of the earth.

As the Phoenix King continued to channel the flame, the ground beneath his feet began to tremble, and the air was filled with a deep, resonant hum. The villagers watched in awe as the flames surged around them, their light and heat filling the village with a sense of hope and renewal.

Finally, after what felt like an eternity, the flames began to settle, their light and heat receding as the Phoenix King completed his task. The village, once reduced to rubble, was now restored, its buildings standing tall and strong, their walls glowing with the energy of the flame. The villagers, once filled with despair, were now filled with hope, their faces glowing with gratitude and joy.

The Phoenix King opened his eyes, his heart filled with a sense of accomplishment and purpose. He had used the power of the Eternal Flame to restore what had been lost, to bring hope and renewal to those who had suffered. But he also knew that the power he had wielded was a great responsibility, that he must always be mindful of the balance between life and death, creation and destruction.

The villagers rushed forward, their eyes filled with gratitude as they bowed before the Phoenix King. "Thank you, Phoenix King," one of the villagers said, her voice trembling with emotion. "You have saved us. You have given us hope when we had none. We will never forget what you have done for us."

The Phoenix King smiled, his heart filled with warmth. "It was my duty," he replied, his voice steady. "The power of the Eternal Flame is a force of creation and destruction, of life and death. It is my responsibility to ensure that this power is used to protect the balance of our world."

Ignis floated beside the Phoenix King, his ember eyes glowing with pride. "You did it, my king," he whispered, his voice crackling with excitement. "You used the power of the Eternal Flame to bring life where there was once only death. You've become a symbol of hope and renewal."

The Phoenix King nodded, his heart filled with resolve. "Yes," he replied, his voice steady. "But I must also remember the burden of this power. I must always ensure that the balance is maintained, that the power of the flame is used wisely and justly."

With that, the Phoenix King and Ignis left the village, their hearts filled with a sense of purpose and determination. The Phoenix King knew that his journey was far from over, that there were still challenges ahead, but he was ready to face them. He had the power of the Eternal Flame within him, and with it, he would protect the balance of Eldoria.

The Burden of Power

As the Phoenix King continued his journey, the weight of his new power began to settle on his shoulders. The ability to resurrect the fallen, to bring life where there was once only death, was a power of immense responsibility. It was a gift, but it was also a burden—a reminder that the balance between life and death, creation and destruction, must always be maintained.

The Phoenix King knew that he could not use this power recklessly. Each time he resurrected someone, he had to ensure that the balance was not disrupted, that the cycle of life and death continued as it was meant to. He understood now that the power of the Eternal Flame was not just about giving life—it was about understanding when to let life end, when to allow the natural order to take its course.

This realization weighed heavily on the Phoenix King, and he began to question the limits of his power. How far could he go without disrupting the balance? How many lives could he save before the consequences became too great? These were questions that had no easy answers, and the Phoenix King knew that he would have to tread carefully, that he would have to rely on his wisdom and understanding of the balance to guide him.

As the Phoenix King pondered these questions, Ignis floated beside him, his ember eyes filled with concern. "You've been quiet, my king," Ignis said, his voice crackling with worry. "Is everything alright?"

The Phoenix King sighed, his heart heavy with the weight of his new responsibility. "I'm just thinking about the power I've gained," he replied, his voice steady. "The ability to resurrect the fallen, to bring life where there was once only death... it's an incredible gift, but it's also a great responsibility. I have to be careful, Ignis. I have to ensure that the balance is maintained."

Ignis nodded, his ember eyes glowing with understanding. "I know, my king," he replied, his voice filled with empathy. "But you've always been wise, always understood the importance of balance. I have faith that you'll use this power wisely."

The Phoenix King smiled, grateful for Ignis's unwavering support. "Thank you, Ignis," he said softly. "I will do my best to protect the balance, to use this power for the greater good."

As they continued their journey, the Phoenix King began to see the world in a new light. The fire within him, the power of the Eternal Flame, allowed him to see the intricate web of energy that connected all things, the cycle of life and death that governed the world. He could see the consequences of his actions, the ripple effects that spread out from each decision he made. It was a sobering realization, but it also gave him a deeper understanding of his role as the guardian of the balance.

The Phoenix King knew that he could not save everyone, that there would be times when he would have to let go, when he would have to allow the natural order to take its course. But he also knew that there would be times when he could make a difference, when he could use his power to bring hope and renewal to those who had lost everything.

It was a delicate balance, a fine line between creation and destruction, life and death. But the Phoenix King was determined to walk that line, to use his power to protect the balance of Eldoria and to ensure that the cycles of life and death continued in harmony.

A Symbol of Hope and Renewal

As the Phoenix King continued his journey, word of his deeds began to spread throughout Eldoria. Tales of the Phoenix King's power, of his ability to resurrect the fallen and to bring life where there was once only death, spread like wildfire, reaching every corner of the land. The Phoenix King became a symbol of hope and renewal, a beacon of light in a world that had known too much darkness.

People from all walks of life sought out the Phoenix King, seeking his help, his guidance, and his blessing. They came to him with their stories of loss and despair, their pleas for help and for hope. And the Phoenix King, mindful of the balance he had sworn to protect, listened to each one, offering what help he could while always ensuring that the balance between life and death was maintained.

The Phoenix King's reputation grew, and soon he became known as the Guardian of the Flame, the protector of the balance, the one who could bring life where there was once only death. But with this newfound fame came new challenges, new burdens that the Phoenix King had not anticipated.

The people of Eldoria began to see the Phoenix King not just as a ruler, but as a savior, someone who could solve all their problems, heal all their wounds, and bring back all that had been lost. They began to place their hopes and dreams on his shoulders, expecting him to be the answer to all their prayers.

The Phoenix King understood their desperation, their need for hope in a world that had known so much suffering. But he also knew that he could not be everything to everyone, that he could not save everyone who came to him. The power of the Eternal Flame was not infinite, and the balance between life and death could not be disrupted without consequences.

This realization weighed heavily on the Phoenix King, and he began to feel the burden of his new role. He knew that he had to be careful, that he had to use his power wisely and justly. But he also knew that he could not turn his back on those who needed him, that he had to find a way to balance his responsibilities as a ruler with his new role as the Guardian of the Flame.

Ignis, always by his side, noticed the Phoenix King's growing burden and spoke up, his voice filled with concern. "My king, you've taken on so much," Ignis said, his ember eyes glowing with empathy. "I can see the weight you're carrying, the burden of your new power. But you don't have to do this alone. There are those who can help you, who can share the burden."

The Phoenix King sighed, his heart heavy with the weight of his responsibilities. "I know, Ignis," he replied, his voice filled with exhaustion. "But I don't want to burden others with my responsibilities. The power of the Eternal Flame is a gift, but it's also a great responsibility. I have to ensure that it's used wisely, that the balance is maintained."

Ignis floated closer, his voice filled with determination. "But you're not alone, my king," he said firmly. "You have allies, friends, people who care about you and who want to help you. You don't have to carry this burden by yourself. Let us help you. Let us share the responsibility."

The Phoenix King looked at Ignis, his heart filled with gratitude. "Thank you, Ignis," he said softly. "You're right. I can't do this alone. I need the support of those around me, the help of those who share my commitment to the balance."

With that realization, the Phoenix King began to reach out to those who could help him, forming alliances with other rulers, wise elders, and skilled warriors who understood the importance of the balance. He shared the burden of his responsibilities, delegating tasks and seeking advice from those who had experience and wisdom to offer.

The Phoenix King's decision to share the burden of his responsibilities proved to be a wise one. With the support of his allies, he was able to manage the demands placed on him, to ensure that the power of the Eternal Flame was used wisely and justly. He became not just a ruler, but a leader, someone who inspired others to take up the cause of protecting the balance.

As the Phoenix King's influence grew, so too did the hope and renewal that he brought to the people of Eldoria. The land began to heal, the wounds of the past began to mend, and the cycles of life and death continued in harmony. The Phoenix King's legacy as the Guardian of the Flame was secured, and he became a symbol of hope and renewal for generations to come.

The Rise to Power

With the power of the Eternal Flame within him and the support of his allies, the Phoenix King's rise to power was complete. He had become more than just a ruler—he had become a symbol of hope and renewal, a guardian of the balance, and a force for good in a world that had known too much darkness.

The Phoenix King's reign was marked by peace and prosperity, by a renewed sense of purpose and unity among the people of Eldoria. The power of the Eternal Flame, used wisely and justly, brought life where there was once only death, healed the wounds of the past, and ensured that the cycles of life and death continued in harmony.

But the Phoenix King never forgot the burden of his power, the responsibility that came with being the Guardian of the Flame. He knew that the balance between creation and destruction, life and death, was delicate, and that it was his duty to protect that balance, to ensure that the power of the flame was used for the greater good.

As the Phoenix King looked out over his kingdom, his heart filled with pride and resolve. He knew that his journey was far from over, that there were still challenges ahead, but he was ready to face them. He had the power of the Eternal Flame within him, and with it, he would protect the balance of Eldoria, ensuring that the cycles of life and death, creation and destruction, continued in harmony.

The legend of the Phoenix King had truly begun, and the world of Eldoria would never be the same again. The Phoenix King had risen to power, not just as a ruler, but as a symbol of hope and renewal, a guardian of the balance, and a force for good in a world that had been forever changed by the flames of rebirth.

Chapter 8: The Wrath of the Volcano God

The Unrest in the Earth

The Phoenix King's reign, marked by peace and prosperity, had begun to bring hope and renewal to the people of Eldoria. The power of the Eternal Flame, which he had absorbed and mastered, allowed him to protect the balance between life and death, creation and destruction. Yet, in the depths of the earth, a powerful and ancient entity stirred, displeased with the Phoenix King's influence.

This entity was the Volcano God, an embodiment of primal fire and destruction, a being as old as the mountains themselves. He had ruled over the volcanic lands for eons, his power rooted in the molten heart of the earth, where lava flowed like blood through the veins of the world. The Volcano God thrived on chaos and destruction, believing that only through the complete annihilation of the old could the new truly emerge. To him, the Phoenix King's efforts to maintain balance were an affront to the natural order as he saw it—a challenge to his dominion.

Deep within the core of the earth, where the heat was unbearable to all but the most ancient of beings, the Volcano God seethed with anger. He had watched from afar as the Phoenix King absorbed the power of the Eternal Flame, unlocking the ability to bring life and hope where there was once only death and despair. This act of renewal and creation was antithetical to everything the Volcano God stood for, and he could not allow it to go unchallenged.

In the heart of his volcanic lair, surrounded by rivers of molten lava and pillars of fire, the Volcano God began to plot his retribution. He was a towering figure, his body made of molten rock and searing flames, his eyes burning with the intensity of a thousand infernos. The earth trembled beneath his feet as he moved, the very mountains bowing to his will.

"The Phoenix King," the Volcano God rumbled, his voice echoing through the caverns of the earth. "A being who dares to challenge the natural order, who seeks to maintain a balance that is against the very essence of fire. He is a threat to my dominion, and he must be destroyed."

The Volcano God's fury was boundless, his desire for destruction insatiable. He knew that the Phoenix King was powerful, that he had absorbed the energy of the Eternal Flame, but the Volcano God believed that the raw power of destruction would always triumph over balance and renewal. To prove this, he would challenge the Phoenix King, and he would not rest until the Phoenix King was reduced to ashes.

As the Volcano God's anger grew, the earth itself began to react. The ground shook with increasing intensity, cracks forming in the earth's surface as lava began to bubble up from the depths. Mountains that had stood tall for centuries began to tremble, their peaks glowing with an ominous red light. The people of Eldoria felt the earth's unrest, their hearts filled with fear as they wondered what could be causing such a disturbance.

In the Phoenix Kingdom, the Phoenix King himself felt the tremors, the heat rising from the earth, and the distant rumble of the mountains. He knew that something was amiss, that a great and terrible force was awakening from its slumber. As he stood at the edge of the Sacred Flame, his heart filled with a sense of foreboding, Ignis floated beside him, his ember eyes glowing with concern.

"My king," Ignis said, his voice crackling with worry. "Do you feel it? The earth... it's angry. Something is stirring deep within the mountains. I fear it's something powerful, something ancient."

The Phoenix King nodded, his gaze fixed on the distant mountains that loomed on the horizon. "I feel it too, Ignis," he replied, his voice steady. "There is a great force awakening, a force of destruction and chaos. We must be prepared for whatever challenges lie ahead."

Ignis floated closer, his voice filled with concern. "What do you think it is, my king? Could it be... the Volcano God?"

The Phoenix King's expression darkened at the mention of the Volcano God, a being of legend who was said to control the very fire that burned within the earth. The Volcano God was known to be a force of pure destruction, a being who reveled in chaos and cared nothing for balance or renewal. If it was indeed the Volcano God who was stirring, then the Phoenix King knew that he would be facing his greatest challenge yet.

"I believe it could be, Ignis," the Phoenix King replied, his voice filled with resolve. "The Volcano God is a force of destruction, a being who believes in the annihilation of the old to make way for the new. He sees my efforts to maintain balance as a threat to his dominion, and he will stop at nothing to destroy me."

Ignis's ember eyes widened with fear. "But the Volcano God is powerful, my king—perhaps even more powerful than you. How can we hope to defeat him?"

The Phoenix King took a deep breath, his heart filled with determination. "We must rely on more than just raw power, Ignis," he said, his voice steady. "The Volcano God believes in destruction over renewal, but we know that true power lies in balance—in the harmony between creation and destruction, life and death. We must use our wisdom, our understanding of the fire, to defeat him without succumbing to the lure of pure destruction."

Ignis nodded, his ember eyes glowing with a mixture of fear and resolve. "I believe in you, my king," he said softly. "We've faced many challenges before, and I know we can face this one too. Together, we will protect the balance of Eldoria."

With that, the Phoenix King and Ignis prepared for the battle that was to come. The earth continued to tremble, the heat rising from the ground as the Volcano God's wrath grew more intense. The Phoenix King knew that the time had come to confront this ancient force of destruction, to protect the balance of their world.

The Challenge

The earth's unrest reached a crescendo as the Phoenix King and Ignis made their way toward the volcanic mountains where the Volcano God resided. The ground beneath their feet was hot and unstable, shifting with the energy of the molten lava that bubbled up from the depths. The sky above was dark and foreboding, filled with thick clouds of ash that blocked out the sun, casting the land in an eerie, red glow.

As they approached the base of the largest volcano, the ground began to shake violently, cracks forming in the earth's surface as rivers of lava erupted from the ground. The air was thick with the scent of sulfur, and the heat was almost unbearable, even for the Phoenix King, who was accustomed to the fire.

Suddenly, a massive figure emerged from the volcano's peak, its form towering over the landscape. The Volcano God had arrived, his body made entirely of molten rock and searing flames, his eyes burning with an intense, fiery light. He was a being of immense power, his presence filling the air with a palpable sense of dread.

The Volcano God let out a deafening roar, the sound echoing through the mountains as the very earth trembled beneath his feet. "Phoenix King!" he bellowed, his voice filled with fury. "You dare to challenge my dominion? You dare to defy the natural order with your pitiful attempts to maintain balance? You are a fool, and I will reduce you to ashes!"

The Phoenix King stood his ground, his gaze steady as he faced the Volcano God. He could feel the heat radiating from the ancient being, the intensity of the flames that made up his body. But he did not waver, his heart filled with resolve.

"I do not seek to challenge your dominion, Volcano God," the Phoenix King replied, his voice calm but firm. "I seek to protect the balance of our world, to ensure that the cycles of life and death, creation and destruction, continue in harmony. Destruction alone is not the answer—it must be balanced with renewal, with the creation of new life."

The Volcano God's eyes narrowed, his molten form seething with rage. "You speak of balance as if it is some noble ideal," he growled, his voice dripping with contempt. "But balance is a lie, a weakness that prevents true power from being realized. Only through complete and utter destruction can the new truly emerge. You are a fool to think that you can defy the natural order with your pitiful notions of renewal."

The Phoenix King remained resolute, his gaze unwavering. "You are wrong, Volcano God," he replied, his voice filled with conviction. "Destruction without renewal is meaningless. It is through the balance of these forces that true power is realized, that the world can continue to thrive. I will not allow you to destroy everything in your quest for power."

The Volcano God let out another roar, the ground beneath his feet cracking as rivers of lava erupted from the earth. "You dare to defy me?" he bellowed, his voice filled with fury. "Very well, Phoenix King. If you wish to protect your precious balance, then you will have to defeat me. But know this—I am the embodiment of fire and destruction, and I will not be easily defeated."

With that, the Volcano God charged toward the Phoenix King, his massive form moving with a speed and ferocity that belied his size. The ground shook with each step he took, the air filled with the sound of crackling flames as the very earth seemed to bend to his will.

The Phoenix King braced himself, his heart pounding with a mixture of fear and determination. He knew that this battle would be his greatest challenge yet, that he would need to use all of his wisdom and newfound powers to defeat the Volcano God without succumbing to the lure of pure destruction.

The Battle Begins

The Phoenix King and the Volcano God clashed with a force that shook the very foundations of the earth. The Volcano God, a being of pure destruction, unleashed torrents of molten lava and searing flames, his power seeming limitless as he sought to overwhelm the Phoenix King with his fury. The ground beneath them cracked and split, rivers of lava erupting from the earth as the two beings of fire and flame battled for dominance.

The Phoenix King, drawing upon the power of the Eternal Flame, met the Volcano God's attacks with his own, his wings ablaze with radiant fire as he countered the onslaught with blasts of pure energy. The flames that surrounded him were not just a force of destruction—they were a force of creation, of renewal, and the Phoenix King wielded them with a precision and control that belied the raw power they held.

As the battle raged on, the Phoenix King could feel the strain of the conflict, the intensity of the Volcano God's attacks pushing him to his limits. The heat was overwhelming, the flames searing his feathers, but he refused to back down. He knew that he could not allow the Volcano God to destroy everything, to reduce Eldoria to a wasteland of ash and molten rock.

But the Phoenix King also knew that he could not simply match the Volcano God's fury with his own. To do so would be to fall into the same trap of pure destruction, to lose sight of the balance that he had sworn to protect. He had to find a way to defeat the Volcano God without succumbing to the same destructive impulses that drove the ancient being.

As the Volcano God unleashed another wave of molten lava, the Phoenix King took to the air, his wings beating against the hot, ash-filled sky. He needed to find a way to turn the tide of the battle, to use his understanding of the balance between creation and destruction to defeat the Volcano God without destroying everything in the process.

Flying high above the battlefield, the Phoenix King surveyed the land below, his mind racing as he considered his options. The Volcano God was a being of immense power, his strength rooted in the very earth itself. But that power was also his weakness—his connection to the earth made him vulnerable to the very forces he sought to control.

The Phoenix King knew that if he could sever that connection, if he could disrupt the Volcano God's link to the molten core of the earth, he could weaken him, make him vulnerable. But doing so would require more than just brute force—it would require wisdom, strategy, and an understanding of the delicate balance between the elements.

With a plan forming in his mind, the Phoenix King descended back to the battlefield, his wings glowing with the light of the Eternal Flame. The Volcano God, seeing his opponent return, let out a roar of fury, his molten body seething with rage.

"You cannot defeat me, Phoenix King!" the Volcano God bellowed, his voice filled with wrath. "I am the embodiment of fire and destruction! You are nothing but a fool who clings to weak notions of balance and renewal!"

The Phoenix King met the Volcano God's gaze, his eyes filled with determination. "You are wrong, Volcano God," he replied, his voice calm but firm. "True power lies not in destruction alone, but in the balance between creation and destruction, life and death. I will show you the strength of that balance."

With that, the Phoenix King unleashed a burst of energy from the Eternal Flame, directing it not at the Volcano God, but at the ground beneath him. The energy surged through the earth, causing the ground to tremble and crack as the Phoenix King disrupted the flow of lava that fed the Volcano God's power.

The Volcano God staggered, his molten body flickering as the flow of energy was disrupted. The connection to the earth that gave him his strength was weakening, the very power he had relied on now working against him.

The Phoenix King saw his opportunity and pressed the advantage, using his control over the fire to redirect the flow of lava away from the Volcano God, cutting off the source of his power. The ground beneath the Volcano God's feet began to cool, the molten rock hardening into solid stone as the Phoenix King exerted his will over the elements.

The Volcano God roared in fury, his massive form trembling as his power began to wane. "What are you doing, Phoenix King?" he bellowed, his voice filled with desperation. "You cannot defeat me! I am the Volcano God, the embodiment of destruction!"

The Phoenix King met the Volcano God's gaze, his eyes filled with resolve. "You are not invincible, Volcano God," he replied, his voice steady. "Your power is rooted in destruction, but that power is meaningless without creation, without renewal. I will not allow you to destroy everything in your quest for power."

With that, the Phoenix King unleashed a final burst of energy, directing it at the heart of the volcano. The ground beneath the Volcano God's feet erupted with light, the energy of the Eternal Flame surging through the earth as the Phoenix King severed the last remaining connection between the Volcano God and the molten core of the earth.

The Volcano God let out a final, deafening roar as his power was stripped away, his massive form collapsing into a heap of molten rock and cooling lava. The ground beneath him solidified, the rivers of lava that had once flowed so freely now reduced to hardened stone.

The battle was over, and the Phoenix King stood victorious, his heart filled with a mixture of relief and resolve. He had defeated the Volcano God, not through pure destruction, but through wisdom and an understanding of the balance that governed all things.

The Aftermath

As the dust settled and the earth began to calm, the Phoenix King looked out over the battlefield, his heart heavy with the weight of what had just transpired. The land, once ravaged by the fury of the Volcano God, was now quiet, the molten rivers reduced to hardened stone, the air filled with the scent of cooling lava.

Ignis floated beside the Phoenix King, his ember eyes glowing with a mixture of awe and concern. "You did it, my king," Ignis said softly, his voice crackling with reverence. "You defeated the Volcano God... but you did so without destroying everything. You maintained the balance."

The Phoenix King nodded, his gaze fixed on the horizon. "Yes," he replied, his voice steady. "But it was not an easy victory. The Volcano God was a being of immense power, and his belief in pure destruction was strong. It would have been easy to fall into the same trap, to match his fury with my own. But that would have only led to more destruction, more chaos."

Ignis floated closer, his voice filled with empathy. "But you didn't succumb to that, my king. You used your wisdom, your understanding of the balance, to defeat him. You've proven that true power lies not in destruction alone, but in the harmony between creation and destruction, life and death."

The Phoenix King looked down at his hands, feeling the energy of the Eternal Flame pulsing through his veins. "Yes," he said softly. "But I must always remember the burden of this power, the responsibility that comes with being the Guardian of the Flame. The balance must be maintained, and I must use this power wisely and justly."

With that, the Phoenix King and Ignis began their journey back to the Phoenix Kingdom, their hearts filled with a sense of purpose and determination. The Phoenix King knew that his battle with the Volcano God was just one of many challenges he would face in his quest to protect the balance of Eldoria. But he also knew that he had the strength, the wisdom, and the resolve to face whatever challenges lay ahead.

As they traveled back to the Phoenix Kingdom, the people of Eldoria began to hear of the Phoenix King's victory over the Volcano God. The tale of his battle spread throughout the land, becoming a legend that would be passed down for generations. The Phoenix King became known as the Guardian of the Flame, a symbol of hope and renewal, a being who had defeated the embodiment of destruction without losing sight of the balance that governed all things.

But the Phoenix King knew that his journey was far from over. There were still many challenges ahead, many battles to be fought, and many decisions to be made. But he was ready to face them, armed with the power of the Eternal

Flame and the knowledge that true power lies not in destruction alone, but in the harmony between creation and destruction, life and death.

And so, the Phoenix King's legend continued to grow, his name becoming synonymous with hope, renewal, and the delicate balance that held the world of Eldoria together. The Phoenix King had risen to power, not just as a ruler, but as a guardian of the balance, a force for good in a world that had been forever changed by the flames of rebirth.

Chapter 9: The Sacrifice

A New Challenge Emerges

The Phoenix King's victory over the Volcano God had brought peace and stability to the land of Eldoria. His reputation as the Guardian of the Flame, a being who protected the balance between creation and destruction, had spread far and wide. Yet, with every victory and every moment of peace, the Phoenix King knew that maintaining the delicate balance of the world would require ongoing vigilance and, perhaps, even greater sacrifices.

In the days following the battle, the Phoenix King began to notice subtle shifts in the world around him. The air felt heavier, the winds colder, and the once vibrant flames that flickered in the Sacred Flame appeared dimmer. It was as if the very essence of life and fire was being sapped from the world, leaving behind a sense of impending dread.

As he stood before the Sacred Flame, contemplating these changes, Ignis, the loyal ember sprite who had been with him through every trial, floated beside him, his ember eyes filled with concern. "My king, something is wrong," Ignis said, his voice crackling with worry. "The flames... they're weaker. I can feel it too. It's as if the balance is slipping away again, despite all we've done."

The Phoenix King nodded, his gaze fixed on the Sacred Flame. "Yes, Ignis, I feel it too," he replied, his voice heavy with concern. "The battle with the Volcano God may have disrupted the balance more than I realized. While we prevented destruction, we may not have fully restored the harmony that the world requires. The balance is delicate, and even the smallest disruption can have far-reaching consequences."

Ignis floated closer, his voice filled with urgency. "What should we do, my king? We've faced so many challenges before, but this feels different. The balance must be restored, or everything we've fought for could be lost."

The Phoenix King sighed, his heart weighed down by the burden of his responsibilities. He knew that maintaining the balance was not just about defeating enemies or quelling natural disasters—it was about understanding the intricate web of life and death, creation and destruction, that governed the world. And sometimes, restoring that balance required making difficult and painful choices.

As the Phoenix King pondered the situation, a sense of unease settled over him. He knew that there was only one way to truly understand what was happening—he would need to consult the ancient scrolls of the Phoenix Kingdom, the sacred texts that contained the knowledge of his ancestors and the secrets of the Eternal Flame.

The Ancient Scrolls and the Prophecy

The ancient scrolls of the Phoenix Kingdom were kept in a hidden chamber deep within the heart of the palace, a place that only the Phoenix King himself could access. These scrolls contained the wisdom of generations past, the knowledge of the Phoenix Kings who had come before him, and the prophecies that foretold the challenges and trials that each Phoenix King would face.

The chamber was a place of reverence, its walls lined with golden flames that flickered gently, casting a warm, ethereal light over the scrolls. The air was thick with the scent of incense, and the ground beneath the Phoenix King's feet was cool and smooth, as if the very stones had been infused with the essence of the Sacred Flame.

As the Phoenix King entered the chamber, he felt a sense of awe and reverence wash over him. The knowledge contained within these scrolls was sacred, passed down through the ages to guide the Phoenix Kings in their quest to protect the balance of the world.

Ignis, floating beside him, looked around the chamber with wide eyes. "This place... it feels so ancient, so full of power," Ignis whispered, his voice crackling with awe. "I've never been here before, my king. What are we looking for?"

The Phoenix King approached the central pedestal, where the most important of the scrolls were kept. "We're looking for answers, Ignis," he replied, his voice steady. "The balance is slipping away, and we need to understand why. The scrolls contain the wisdom of our ancestors—they may hold the key to restoring the harmony we've lost."

With great care, the Phoenix King unrolled one of the scrolls, his eyes scanning the ancient text. The scroll was written in the language of the Phoenix, a language known only to the rulers of the Phoenix Kingdom, passed down from generation to generation. As he read the words, the Phoenix King felt a chill run down his spine.

The scroll spoke of a prophecy, a time when the balance of the world would be threatened by a great disruption—an imbalance so severe that it could only be corrected through a sacrifice of great importance. The text was cryptic, filled with metaphors and symbols, but the message was clear: to restore the balance, something dear to the Phoenix King would need to be sacrificed.

The Phoenix King's heart sank as he realized the gravity of the situation. The prophecy was not just a warning—it was a directive. To maintain the balance, he would need to give up something precious, something that held great meaning to him. But what could that be? What could possibly be so important that its loss would restore the balance?

Ignis, sensing the Phoenix King's distress, floated closer, his ember eyes filled with concern. "What does it say, my king?" Ignis asked softly. "What do we need to do?"

The Phoenix King hesitated for a moment before replying, his voice heavy with sorrow. "The scrolls speak of a prophecy, Ignis—a time when the balance of the world would be threatened by a great disruption. It says that to restore the balance, a sacrifice must be made... something dear to me, something precious."

Ignis's ember eyes widened with fear. "A sacrifice? But... what could that mean? What could you possibly sacrifice that would restore the balance?"

The Phoenix King shook his head, his heart filled with uncertainty. "I don't know, Ignis. But I fear that whatever it is, it will be a difficult and painful decision. The balance must be maintained, but at what cost?"

As the Phoenix King and Ignis pondered the meaning of the prophecy, a heavy silence settled over the chamber. The flames that lined the walls flickered gently, their light casting long shadows that danced across the ancient scrolls. The Phoenix King knew that he would need to make a choice—a choice that could determine the fate of the world.

A Painful Realization

Days passed as the Phoenix King wrestled with the prophecy and the knowledge that a sacrifice would be required to restore the balance. He sought counsel from the wise elders of the Phoenix Kingdom, meditated before the Sacred Flame, and even ventured into the depths of the earth where the remnants of the Volcano God's power still lingered. But no matter where he turned, the answer eluded him.

The Phoenix King's heart grew heavier with each passing day, the weight of his responsibilities pressing down on him like a crushing burden. He knew that the balance of the world was slipping further out of reach, and the longer he delayed, the greater the consequences would be.

Ignis, always by his side, watched the Phoenix King with growing concern. He could see the toll that the prophecy was taking on his beloved king, the strain of carrying the fate of the world on his shoulders. And though Ignis was small, a mere ember sprite, he felt a deep and abiding loyalty to the Phoenix King—a loyalty that would soon lead him to make the most difficult decision of his existence.

One evening, as the sun set over the Phoenix Kingdom, casting the land in a warm, golden light, the Phoenix King sat alone on a high cliff overlooking the kingdom. The wind whipped through his feathers, carrying with it the distant sound of crackling flames from the Sacred Flame below. The weight of the prophecy was heavy on his heart, and he felt more alone than ever.

Ignis, sensing the Phoenix King's despair, floated beside him, his ember eyes glowing with a mixture of empathy and determination. "My king," Ignis said softly, his voice crackling with emotion. "I know this is hard for you, but you don't have to carry this burden alone. We've faced so many challenges together, and we've always found a way. I know we can find a way this time too."

The Phoenix King looked at Ignis, his heart filled with gratitude for the loyal companion who had been with him through every trial. "Thank you, Ignis," he replied, his voice heavy with sorrow. "But this time... it feels different. The prophecy is clear—a sacrifice must be made, and I don't know what that sacrifice should be. I fear that whatever I choose, it will come at a great cost."

Ignis floated closer, his ember eyes filled with a deep, unwavering resolve. "My king... I've been thinking," Ignis began, his voice trembling slightly. "I've been thinking about the prophecy, about the balance, and... about the sacrifice."

The Phoenix King's heart skipped a beat as he looked at Ignis, a sense of dread filling him. "What are you saying, Ignis?" he asked, his voice filled with apprehension.

Ignis hesitated for a moment, his ember eyes flickering with uncertainty. But then he took a deep breath, his resolve strengthening. "My king... I believe that I am the sacrifice," Ignis said, his voice filled with a quiet determination. "I'm the one who is dear to you, the one who is precious. If my sacrifice can restore the balance, then it's what I must do."

The Phoenix King's eyes widened in shock and disbelief. "No, Ignis!" he exclaimed, his voice filled with anguish. "I won't let you do this! You've been with me through everything—you've been my companion, my friend. I won't lose you, not like this!"

Ignis floated closer, his voice filled with a gentle but firm resolve. "My king, please listen to me," Ignis said softly. "I've thought about this long and hard, and I believe it's the right thing to do. The balance of the world is more important than any one of us, even me. If my sacrifice can restore that balance, then it's a sacrifice worth making."

The Phoenix King's heart ached with the weight of Ignis's words. He knew that Ignis was right, that the balance of the world was paramount, but the thought of losing his loyal companion was too much to bear. The Phoenix King had faced many challenges, but none had been as painful as this—choosing between the fate of the world and the life of someone he held dear.

"Ignis... I can't do this," the Phoenix King said, his voice trembling with emotion. "I can't ask you to sacrifice yourself for the sake of the balance. There must be another way."

Ignis floated closer still, his ember eyes glowing with a deep, abiding love for the Phoenix King. "You're not asking, my king," Ignis replied gently. "I'm offering. You've always protected the balance, always put the needs of the world above your own. Now it's my turn to do the same. Please, let me do this. Let me help you one last time."

The Phoenix King's heart shattered at Ignis's words, tears welling up in his eyes as he realized the painful truth. Ignis was right—the balance of the world was more important than any one life, even the life of someone as dear as Ignis. The Phoenix King knew that he had no choice but to accept Ignis's offer, to perform the ritual that would restore the balance, even if it meant losing his closest friend.

With a heavy heart, the Phoenix King nodded, his voice choked with emotion. "Very well, Ignis," he said softly. "If this is truly what you want, then I will honor your sacrifice. But know that this is the hardest decision I have ever had to make. You have been my loyal companion, my friend, and I will never forget you."

Ignis floated closer, his ember eyes filled with a gentle warmth. "Thank you, my king," Ignis replied, his voice filled with love. "I'm honored to have served you, and I'm proud to make this sacrifice for the greater good. I know you will continue to protect the balance, and I will always be with you in spirit."

With that, the Phoenix King and Ignis prepared for the ritual that would restore the balance of the world—a ritual that would require the ultimate sacrifice.

The Ritual of Sacrifice

The ritual to restore the balance was an ancient and sacred ceremony, one that had been performed only a few times in the history of the Phoenix Kingdom. It required a place of great power, where the forces of creation and destruction, life and death, converged in perfect harmony. The Phoenix King knew that there was only one place in Eldoria that met these criteria—the Heart of the Mountain, where the Eternal Flame had been born.

The journey to the Heart of the Mountain was a solemn one, filled with a sense of finality and purpose. The Phoenix King and Ignis traveled in silence, the weight of what was to come pressing down on them like a heavy shroud. The land around them was quiet, the air filled with a stillness that seemed to echo the gravity of the situation.

As they approached the entrance to the mountain, the ground beneath their feet began to tremble, the air growing hotter as they neared the molten core of the earth. The flames that had once danced so brightly in the Phoenix King's presence now flickered weakly, as if the very essence of fire itself was mourning the loss that was to come.

Ignis floated beside the Phoenix King, his ember eyes filled with a mixture of determination and sadness. "This is it, my king," Ignis said softly, his voice crackling with emotion. "The Heart of the Mountain. It's the perfect place for the ritual."

The Phoenix King nodded, his heart heavy with sorrow. "Yes, Ignis," he replied, his voice filled with grief. "It's the place where the Eternal Flame was born, where the forces of creation and destruction are in perfect balance. It's the only place where the ritual can be performed."

As they entered the Heart of the Mountain, the ground beneath their feet glowed with a radiant, golden light. The walls of the chamber were lined with glowing crystals that pulsed with the energy of the fire that burned within the mountain's core. In the center of the chamber, a massive, glowing flame burned, its light filling the room with a sense of peace and tranquility.

The Phoenix King and Ignis approached the flame, their hearts filled with a mixture of reverence and sorrow. They knew that this was the moment of truth, the moment when the balance of the world would be restored, but at a great and terrible cost.

The Phoenix King took a deep breath, his voice trembling as he spoke the words of the ancient ritual. "I stand before the Eternal Flame, the source of creation and destruction, life and death," he began, his voice filled with reverence. "I seek to restore the balance of the world, to ensure that the cycles of life and death, creation and destruction, continue in harmony. To do this, I offer a sacrifice—a sacrifice of great importance, a sacrifice of something dear to me."

Ignis floated beside the Phoenix King, his ember eyes glowing with a gentle warmth. "I, Ignis, offer myself as the sacrifice," Ignis said softly, his voice filled with love. "I offer my life to restore the balance, to ensure that the world continues in harmony. I do this willingly, knowing that it is for the greater good."

The Phoenix King's heart ached with the weight of Ignis's words, tears streaming down his face as he realized the full extent of the sacrifice that was about to be made. He knew that he had to go through with it, that the balance of the world depended on it, but the thought of losing Ignis was almost too much to bear.

With a heavy heart, the Phoenix King raised his hand, his fingers glowing with the light of the Eternal Flame. He placed his hand on Ignis's small, glowing form, his voice choked with emotion as he spoke the final words of the ritual.

"I accept your sacrifice, Ignis," the Phoenix King said softly, his voice trembling with grief. "May your light live on in the balance of the world, and may your spirit always be with me."

As the Phoenix King spoke the final words of the ritual, the light of the Eternal Flame flared to life, its radiant glow filling the chamber with an intense, blinding light. The ground beneath their feet trembled, the air filled with a deep, resonant hum as the forces of creation and destruction, life and death, converged in perfect harmony.

The Phoenix King could feel the energy of the flame surging through him, resonating with the fire within him as the ritual reached its climax. Ignis's small, glowing form began to fade, his ember eyes filled with a gentle warmth as he looked at the Phoenix King one last time.

"Goodbye, my king," Ignis whispered, his voice filled with love. "Thank you... for everything."

With those final words, Ignis's form dissolved into the light of the Eternal Flame, his essence merging with the fire that burned at the heart of the mountain. The chamber was filled with a blinding light, the air thick with the scent of molten rock and burning incense as the ritual was completed.

The Phoenix King stood alone in the chamber, his heart shattered by the loss of his loyal companion. The light of the Eternal Flame gradually dimmed, returning to its normal, steady glow as the forces of creation and destruction, life and death, settled into their natural balance once more.

The balance had been restored, but at a great cost. The Phoenix King had lost something dear to him, something precious, and the pain of that loss would stay with him for the rest of his life.

The Aftermath

As the Phoenix King left the Heart of the Mountain, the weight of Ignis's sacrifice pressed heavily on his heart. The world around him had regained its balance—the flames burned brightly once more, the earth was steady and calm, and the winds carried the gentle warmth of the fire—but the Phoenix King felt a deep and abiding sorrow within him.

The people of Eldoria rejoiced at the restoration of the balance, grateful for the peace and stability that had returned to their land. They hailed the Phoenix King as a hero, a guardian of the flame who had protected the world from destruction. But the Phoenix King could not share in their joy, for he knew that the cost of maintaining the balance had been too high.

Days turned into weeks, and the Phoenix King continued to rule his kingdom with wisdom and justice, always mindful of the delicate balance that he had sworn to protect. But the loss of Ignis weighed heavily on his heart, a constant reminder of the sacrifices that came with the power he wielded.

The Phoenix King knew that the balance of the world was a fragile thing, that it required constant vigilance and care. He understood now more than ever that true power lay not in raw strength or destruction, but in the harmony between creation and destruction, life and death. And he knew that sometimes, maintaining that balance required making difficult and painful choices.

But the Phoenix King also knew that he could not allow himself to be consumed by grief. He had a responsibility to his people, to the world, and to the memory of Ignis, to continue his work as the Guardian of the Flame. He would honor Ignis's sacrifice by protecting the balance, by ensuring that the cycles of life and death, creation and destruction, continued in harmony.

And so, the Phoenix King rose each day with renewed resolve, his heart filled with a quiet determination to fulfill his duty. He knew that the road ahead would not be easy, that there would be more challenges and sacrifices to come, but he was ready to face them.

For the Phoenix King had learned a painful lesson about the cost of power, a lesson that would stay with him for the rest of his life. But he had also learned that the greatest power of all was the power to protect the balance, to ensure that the world continued to thrive in harmony.

And as the Phoenix King looked out over his kingdom, the flames of the Sacred Flame burning brightly in the distance, he knew that Ignis's spirit would always be with him, guiding him, supporting him, and reminding him of the true meaning of sacrifice.

The legend of the Phoenix King continued to grow, his name becoming synonymous with hope, renewal, and the delicate balance that held the world of Eldoria together. The Phoenix King had risen to power, not just as a ruler, but as a guardian of the balance, a force for good in a world that had been forever changed by the flames of sacrifice.

Chapter 10: The Phoenix King's Ascension

The Return to the Phoenix Kingdom

The journey back to the Phoenix Kingdom was a bittersweet one for the Phoenix King. The victory over the Volcano God and the painful sacrifice of Ignis had restored the balance of the world, but the cost had been high. The Phoenix King carried the weight of these events with him as he made his way home, the lessons learned through his trials deeply etched into his soul.

As he approached the boundaries of the Phoenix Kingdom, the landscape began to change. The once tumultuous skies had cleared, giving way to a brilliant azure expanse. The land, which had been ravaged by the disruption in balance, now blossomed with new life. Flowers bloomed in vibrant colors, trees stood tall and strong, and the rivers ran clear and fresh. It was as if the very essence of the Phoenix King's power had breathed new life into the world, bringing prosperity and renewal.

The people of the Phoenix Kingdom had eagerly awaited their king's return. News of his battles and the sacrifices he had made spread like wildfire, and the anticipation of his homecoming grew with each passing day. They prepared for his arrival with reverence and excitement, knowing that the Phoenix King's return signified the dawn of a new era—an era of peace, balance, and prosperity.

As the Phoenix King crossed the final threshold into his kingdom, the people gathered to greet him, their faces alight with joy and gratitude. They lined the streets, cheering and waving banners emblazoned with the symbol of the Phoenix—a majestic bird rising from the flames, a symbol of rebirth and renewal. The sight filled the Phoenix King's heart with a mixture of pride and humility, for he knew that his people were not just celebrating his return; they were celebrating the hope and stability that he had fought so hard to secure.

Ignis had once been by his side for such moments, but now, the Phoenix King walked alone, his loyal companion's spirit living on in his heart. The absence was palpable, a quiet reminder of the price of leadership, but the Phoenix King knew that Ignis's sacrifice had not been in vain. It had ensured the continuation of the balance and the flourishing of the kingdom.

As the Phoenix King made his way through the throngs of people, he acknowledged them with a nod and a smile, his presence commanding respect and admiration. The citizens of the Phoenix Kingdom looked upon their king with reverence, seeing in him not just a ruler, but a guardian who had faced unimaginable challenges and emerged stronger, wiser, and more determined than ever to protect his people.

The path through the kingdom led to the grand palace, a structure that had stood for centuries, its towering spires reaching toward the sky, symbolizing the kingdom's connection to the heavens. The palace, much like the kingdom itself, had undergone a transformation. The once faded and weathered stones now gleamed with a renewed brilliance, as if the very walls had absorbed the power of the Eternal Flame.

At the entrance to the palace, the Phoenix King was met by the council of elders, wise and venerable figures who had served as advisors to the kings of the past. They bowed deeply before the Phoenix King, their expressions filled with respect and admiration.

"Welcome home, my king," said the eldest of the council, his voice filled with warmth. "You have brought honor and glory to our kingdom. The trials you have faced, the sacrifices you have made—they have not gone unnoticed. The people of the Phoenix Kingdom are forever in your debt."

The Phoenix King inclined his head in acknowledgment, his voice humble as he replied. "Thank you, Elder. The journey has been long and difficult, but it has been worth every challenge to see our kingdom restored to its former glory. I could not have done it without the support and faith of my people."

The elder smiled, his eyes twinkling with pride. "You have proven yourself to be a true ruler, Phoenix King. You have demonstrated the wisdom, courage, and compassion that are the hallmarks of a great leader. It is time for you to take your place upon the throne, to guide us into a new era of peace and prosperity."

The Phoenix King nodded, his heart filled with a sense of purpose. He knew that the time had come to fully embrace his role as the ruler of the Phoenix Kingdom, to lead his people with the strength and wisdom he had gained through his trials. The journey had prepared him for this moment, and he was ready to ascend to the throne.

Preparations for the Coronation

The coronation of the Phoenix King was a momentous event, one that had been eagerly anticipated by the people of the Phoenix Kingdom. It was not just a ceremony; it was a symbol of the new era that was about to begin, an era of balance, prosperity, and renewal. The preparations for the coronation began immediately, with every detail meticulously planned to reflect the significance of the occasion.

The grand hall of the palace, where the coronation was to take place, was transformed into a spectacle of beauty and grandeur. The walls were adorned with tapestries depicting the history of the Phoenix Kingdom, from its founding to the present day. The ceiling, a vast expanse of polished stone, was painted with images of the Phoenix rising from the flames, a powerful symbol of rebirth and renewal.

The throne, a magnificent seat carved from the finest marble and inlaid with gold and precious gems, was placed at the far end of the hall. It was a symbol of the Phoenix King's authority and the power of the Eternal Flame, a reminder of the responsibilities that came with the crown. The throne had been passed down through generations of Phoenix Kings, each ruler adding their own mark to the legacy of the kingdom.

The hall was filled with flowers and greenery, symbols of life and growth, representing the new beginning that the Phoenix King's ascension would bring. The air was filled with the scent of blooming flowers and the sound of gentle music, creating an atmosphere of peace and tranquility.

As the day of the coronation approached, the people of the Phoenix Kingdom gathered from all corners of the land to witness the event. Nobles, warriors, scholars, and commoners alike filled the grand hall, their faces filled with anticipation and excitement. It was a day that would be remembered for generations, a day when the Phoenix King would take his place upon the throne and lead his people into a new era.

The Phoenix King, dressed in ceremonial robes of crimson and gold, stood before the council of elders, his heart filled with a sense of purpose and resolve. He had faced many challenges on his journey, but this was the culmination of everything he had learned, everything he had fought for. He was ready to take his place as the ruler of the Phoenix Kingdom, to guide his people with wisdom, strength, and compassion.

The elder who had welcomed him home stepped forward, holding the ancient crown of the Phoenix Kings in his hands. The crown was a work of art, crafted from the finest gold and adorned with precious gems that sparkled in the light. At its center was a large, flawless ruby, a symbol of the Eternal Flame that burned at the heart of the kingdom.

The elder raised the crown high, his voice filled with reverence as he spoke. "Phoenix King, you have proven yourself worthy of this crown. You have demonstrated the qualities of a true ruler—wisdom, courage, and compassion. You have faced unimaginable trials and emerged stronger and wiser. It is with great honor that we bestow upon you the crown of the Phoenix Kings, and with it, the responsibilities of leadership."

With those words, the elder placed the crown upon the Phoenix King's head, the weight of the ancient symbol settling on his brow. The moment the crown touched his head, the room was filled with a brilliant light, as if the very essence of the Eternal Flame had been ignited within the hall.

The people of the Phoenix Kingdom erupted in cheers and applause, their voices echoing through the grand hall as they celebrated the ascension of their king. The sound was deafening, a chorus of joy and hope that filled the room with energy and excitement.

The Phoenix King stood tall and proud, his heart filled with a sense of fulfillment and purpose. He had been crowned as the ruler of the Phoenix Kingdom, and with that title came the responsibility to protect and guide his people, to ensure that the balance of the world was maintained.

The Coronation Ceremony

The coronation ceremony was a grand and elaborate affair, filled with symbolism and tradition. The entire kingdom had come together to celebrate the ascension of their king, and every detail of the ceremony had been carefully planned to reflect the significance of the occasion.

The grand hall was filled with the nobility of the kingdom, their finest garments adorned with the colors and symbols of their houses. The air was thick with anticipation, as the assembled crowd awaited the moment when their king would take his place upon the throne.

At the head of the hall stood the throne itself, a magnificent seat of power that had been passed down through generations of Phoenix Kings. It was adorned with symbols of fire and renewal, a reminder of the responsibilities that came with the crown.

As the ceremony began, the elder who had placed the crown upon the Phoenix King's head stepped forward, his voice ringing out clearly in the grand hall. "People of the Phoenix Kingdom, we gather here today to witness the coronation of our king, a ruler who has proven himself worthy of the crown through his deeds, his wisdom, and his compassion."

The elder paused for a moment, allowing his words to sink in before continuing. "The Phoenix King has faced many challenges, both within our kingdom and beyond. He has demonstrated the strength of his character and the depth of his wisdom. He has protected the balance of our world and ensured that the cycles of life and death, creation and destruction, continue in harmony."

As the elder spoke, the assembled crowd listened in rapt attention, their faces filled with reverence and respect for the man who was now their king.

"Today, we celebrate not just the coronation of a king, but the beginning of a new era," the elder continued. "An era of peace, prosperity, and renewal. The Phoenix King has brought balance to our world, and he will guide us into a future filled with hope and promise."

With those words, the elder stepped aside, and the Phoenix King stepped forward, his heart filled with a sense of purpose and resolve. He looked out over the assembled crowd, the faces of his people filled with anticipation and hope. He knew that this was his moment, the moment when he would take his place as the ruler of the Phoenix Kingdom and lead his people into a new era.

The Phoenix King raised his hands, and the room fell silent, the anticipation palpable in the air. "People of the Phoenix Kingdom," he began, his voice strong and steady. "I stand before you today not just as your king, but as your servant. I have taken the crown, but with it comes the responsibility to protect and guide our kingdom, to ensure that the balance of our world is maintained."

The Phoenix King paused for a moment, his gaze sweeping across the crowd. "We have faced many challenges, and there will be more to come. But together, we will overcome them. Together, we will build a kingdom that is strong, prosperous, and in harmony with the world around us. I vow to lead you with wisdom, strength, and compassion, and to protect the balance that is so vital to our survival."

As the Phoenix King finished speaking, the room erupted in cheers and applause, the sound filling the grand hall with energy and excitement. The people of the Phoenix Kingdom celebrated their king, their voices echoing through the palace as they hailed the beginning of a new era.

The elder stepped forward once more, a ceremonial staff in his hands. "Phoenix King, as a symbol of your authority and your commitment to the balance of our world, I present to you the Staff of Renewal," the elder said, his voice filled with reverence. "This staff has been passed down through generations of Phoenix Kings, a symbol of the power of the Eternal Flame and the responsibility of leadership."

The Phoenix King accepted the staff, feeling the weight of the ancient symbol in his hands. The staff was a work of art, crafted from the finest wood and inlaid with gold and precious gems. At its top was a large, flawless crystal that glowed with a soft, warm light—a reminder of the Eternal Flame that burned at the heart of the kingdom.

The elder smiled, his eyes twinkling with pride. "With this staff, you will lead our kingdom into a new era. You will protect the balance of our world and ensure that the cycles of life and death, creation and destruction, continue in harmony."

The Phoenix King nodded, his heart filled with a sense of fulfillment and purpose. He knew that the journey ahead would be difficult, but he was ready to face whatever challenges lay before him. He had been crowned as the ruler of the Phoenix Kingdom, and with that title came the responsibility to protect and guide his people.

The Beginning of a New Era

With the coronation complete, the Phoenix King took his place upon the throne, the Staff of Renewal in his hands and the crown of the Phoenix Kings upon his brow. The grand hall was filled with the light of the Eternal Flame, its warmth and energy filling the room with a sense of peace and tranquility.

The people of the Phoenix Kingdom looked upon their king with reverence and admiration, knowing that they were witnessing the beginning of a new era—an era of balance, prosperity, and renewal. The Phoenix King had proven himself to be a wise and just ruler, and they had faith that he would lead them into a future filled with hope and promise.

As the days turned into weeks and the weeks into months, the Phoenix King set about the task of governing his kingdom. He worked tirelessly to ensure that the balance of the world was maintained, that the cycles of life and death, creation and destruction, continued in harmony.

The Phoenix Kingdom flourished under his rule, its people living in peace and prosperity. The land, once ravaged by the disruptions in balance, now blossomed with new life. The rivers ran clear, the forests were filled with the sound of birdsong, and the fields yielded abundant harvests.

The Phoenix King's wisdom and compassion were evident in every decision he made. He listened to the counsel of the elders, sought the advice of his people, and always acted in the best interests of the kingdom. His reign was marked by fairness and justice, and the people of the Phoenix Kingdom prospered under his leadership.

But the Phoenix King never forgot the lessons he had learned on his journey. He knew that power came with a price, and that the balance of the world was a fragile thing that required constant vigilance. He remained humble, always mindful of the responsibilities that came with the crown.

The memory of Ignis, his loyal companion, lived on in his heart. The sacrifice that Ignis had made to restore the balance was a constant reminder of the cost of power, and the Phoenix King honored that sacrifice by leading with wisdom and compassion.

The legend of the Phoenix King continued to grow, his name becoming synonymous with hope, renewal, and the delicate balance that held the world of Eldoria together. The people of the Phoenix Kingdom looked to their king with pride and admiration, knowing that they were in the hands of a ruler who would protect and guide them through any challenge.

And so, the Phoenix King's ascension marked the beginning of a new era—an era of peace, prosperity, and balance. The world of Eldoria was forever changed by the flames of the Eternal Flame, and the Phoenix King's legacy would be remembered for generations to come.

The Phoenix King had risen to power, not just as a ruler, but as a guardian of the balance, a force for good in a world that had been forever changed by the flames of renewal. And as he sat upon the throne, the Staff of Renewal in his hands and the crown of the Phoenix Kings upon his brow, the Phoenix King knew that he was ready to lead his people into a future filled with hope, promise, and endless possibilities.

Chapter 11: The Council of the Flames

The Formation of the Council

The Phoenix King had ascended to the throne, bringing with him a new era of peace, prosperity, and balance to the Phoenix Kingdom. His wisdom, strength, and compassion had earned him the respect and admiration of his people, and under his rule, the kingdom flourished. However, the Phoenix King knew that to maintain the delicate balance between life and death, creation and destruction, he could not rule alone. He needed the counsel of wise beings who understood the complexities of the world and could help him govern with fairness and justice.

With this in mind, the Phoenix King began to form a council, a group of trusted advisors who would assist him in the governance of the kingdom and the protection of the balance. This council, known as the Council of the Flames, would be composed of beings who embodied the different aspects of fire and life, representing the diverse forces that shaped the world of Eldoria.

The first to be invited to the council were the fire giants, powerful beings who had once guarded the entrance to the mountain where the Eternal Flame resided. These giants, who had tested the Phoenix King's worthiness through a series of trials, had since become his allies, recognizing his commitment to the balance and his understanding of the fire's dual nature. The fire giants were ancient beings, their knowledge and experience spanning centuries, and their presence on the council would bring strength and wisdom to the deliberations.

Next were the fire dragons, the ancient and wise creatures who had challenged the Phoenix King to prove his purity of heart during his quest for the Eternal Flame. These dragons, who had watched over the flame for eons, were embodiments of the elemental forces of fire, possessing a deep understanding of the balance between destruction and renewal. The dragons had seen the rise and fall of civilizations, and their insights would be invaluable in guiding the Phoenix King as he sought to protect the kingdom.

In addition to the fire giants and dragons, the Phoenix King also invited representatives from the various regions of the kingdom, including the elders of the Phoenix Kingdom, wise scholars, and skilled warriors. Each member of the council brought with them a unique perspective, their knowledge and experience contributing to the collective wisdom of the group. The Phoenix King knew that by bringing together such a diverse group of advisors, he would be better equipped to make decisions that would ensure the continued prosperity and balance of the kingdom.

The council met in a grand chamber within the Phoenix King's palace, a room specially designed to accommodate the diverse beings who made up its membership. The chamber was vast, its walls lined with glowing crystals that pulsed with the energy of the Eternal Flame. The ceiling, a dome of polished stone, was adorned with images of the Phoenix and other fire-related symbols, representing the unity and strength of the council.

At the center of the chamber was a large, circular table made of polished obsidian, its surface reflecting the light of the flames that burned in the torches lining the walls. The table was symbolic, representing the equality of all members of the council and the importance of collaboration in maintaining the balance.

The first meeting of the Council of the Flames was a momentous occasion, filled with anticipation and a sense of purpose. The Phoenix King, dressed in his royal robes and wearing the crown of the Phoenix Kings, took his place at the head of the table, the Staff of Renewal in his hand. The other members of the council took their seats, their expressions solemn and respectful as they prepared to discuss the matters of the kingdom.

The Phoenix King looked around the table, his heart filled with gratitude for the beings who had agreed to serve on the council. "My friends," he began, his voice strong and steady. "I have called you here today to form the Council of the Flames, a group of trusted advisors who will help me govern our kingdom and protect the balance of our world. Each of you brings with you a unique perspective, and together, we will work to ensure that the cycles of life and death, creation and destruction, continue in harmony."

The fire giant leader, a towering figure with a body of molten rock and flames, spoke first. His voice was deep and resonant, echoing through the chamber. "Phoenix King, we are honored to serve on this council. We have seen your strength and wisdom, and we know that you are committed to protecting the balance. The fire giants stand ready to assist you in any way we can."

The elder fire dragon, a majestic creature with scales that shimmered like molten gold, nodded in agreement. His voice was soft yet powerful, carrying the weight of centuries of knowledge. "The fire dragons have watched over the Eternal Flame for eons, and we understand the importance of maintaining the balance between destruction and renewal. We will share our wisdom with the council and work to ensure that the kingdom remains prosperous."

The other members of the council, including the elders, scholars, and warriors, also voiced their commitment to the Phoenix King's vision. They spoke of their respect for his leadership and their willingness to work together to protect the kingdom and its people.

The Phoenix King smiled, his heart filled with a sense of purpose and resolve. "Thank you, my friends," he said. "Together, we will ensure that our kingdom remains strong and prosperous, that the balance is maintained, and that our people continue to thrive. Let us begin our work."

With those words, the Council of the Flames was officially formed, and the work of governing the Phoenix Kingdom began.

The First Challenge

The Council of the Flames quickly established itself as a vital part of the Phoenix Kingdom's governance. The members met regularly to discuss matters of importance, from managing the kingdom's resources to addressing the needs of its people. The fire giants and dragons shared their wisdom on maintaining the balance, while the elders, scholars, and warriors provided insights on practical matters and the day-to-day challenges facing the kingdom.

The Phoenix King, who had always valued collaboration and diverse perspectives, found the council to be an invaluable source of guidance. With their help, he was able to make decisions that were fair and just, ensuring that the kingdom remained prosperous and in harmony with the natural world.

However, it wasn't long before the council faced its first true test. An ancient evil, long thought to be dormant, began to stir in the far reaches of the kingdom—a force of darkness that threatened to disrupt the delicate balance the Phoenix King had worked so hard to protect.

It began with whispers—rumors of strange occurrences in the northern mountains, where the land was wild and untamed. Travelers spoke of eerie lights in the sky, of shadows that moved on their own, and of a growing sense of dread that permeated the air. The people of the northern villages, once peaceful and prosperous, began to experience strange phenomena—crops failing, animals disappearing, and the earth itself trembling as if in fear.

The Phoenix King, concerned by these reports, called an emergency meeting of the Council of the Flames. The members gathered in the grand chamber, their expressions grim as they prepared to discuss the growing threat.

As the meeting began, the Phoenix King addressed the council, his voice filled with concern. "My friends, I have received troubling reports from the northern mountains. There are signs that an ancient evil, long thought to be dormant, is beginning to stir. The balance of our world is at risk, and we must act quickly to prevent this threat from spreading."

The fire giant leader, who had faced many battles in his long life, nodded solemnly. "Phoenix King, I have heard of this evil before. It is an ancient force, older than the mountains themselves. It thrives on chaos and destruction, feeding on the fear and suffering of others. If it is truly awakening, we must be prepared for a difficult battle."

The elder fire dragon, who had witnessed the rise and fall of many civilizations, added his voice to the discussion. "This evil is not to be underestimated. It has the power to corrupt and twist the very fabric of reality, turning even the strongest of beings against themselves. We must approach this threat with caution, for it has the potential to unravel the balance we have worked so hard to maintain."

The Phoenix King listened intently to the counsel of the giants and dragons, his mind racing as he considered their words. He knew that this was a challenge unlike any he had faced before—a threat that could not be defeated through sheer force alone. It would require wisdom, strategy, and a deep understanding of the balance between light and darkness.

One of the scholars, a wise elder who had spent his life studying the ancient texts, spoke up, his voice filled with urgency. "Phoenix King, there are ancient prophecies that speak of this evil. The texts warn of a time when the balance of the world would be threatened by a force of darkness, a time when even the strongest of rulers would be tested. The prophecies suggest that the only way to defeat this evil is to confront it directly, to face it with courage and resolve."

The Phoenix King nodded, his heart heavy with the weight of the challenge before him. "Thank you, Elder," he said. "Your words confirm what I have feared. We must confront this evil, but we must do so with care. We cannot allow it to spread, but we must also ensure that we do not disrupt the balance in our efforts to defeat it."

The council members exchanged concerned glances, their expressions reflecting the gravity of the situation. They knew that this was a challenge that would test their strength, their wisdom, and their resolve—a challenge that could determine the fate of the kingdom.

The Phoenix King looked around the table, his gaze meeting that of each council member. "We are facing a great and terrible threat," he said, his voice filled with determination. "But we are not without hope. We have faced challenges before, and we have overcome them through our strength, our wisdom, and our unity. I believe that together, we can confront this evil and protect the balance of our world."

The fire giant leader, his expression resolute, spoke for the council. "We stand with you, Phoenix King. We will face this evil together, and we will do whatever it takes to protect our kingdom and our people."

The elder fire dragon, his voice filled with wisdom, added his support. "We must proceed with caution, but we must also act decisively. The balance of our world is at stake, and we cannot afford to falter."

The Phoenix King nodded, his heart filled with resolve. "Then it is decided. We will confront this evil, and we will do so with all the strength and wisdom at our disposal. Let us prepare for the battle ahead."

With those words, the council began to plan their strategy, working together to devise a plan that would allow them to confront the ancient evil without disrupting the balance of the world. They knew that the road ahead would be difficult, but they were determined to face the challenge head-on.

Confronting the Ancient Evil

The days that followed were filled with preparations as the council made ready to confront the ancient evil. The fire giants, with their immense strength and knowledge of the mountains, took the lead in fortifying the northern villages, building defenses and preparing the people for the possibility of an attack. The fire dragons, with their mastery of the elemental forces, patrolled the skies, watching for any signs of the growing darkness.

The Phoenix King, guided by the wisdom of the council, focused on understanding the nature of the evil they were facing. He spent hours poring over ancient texts and consulting with the elders, seeking any clues that might help them in their battle. He knew that the key to defeating the evil lay in understanding its weaknesses, in finding a way to counter its corrupting influence without disrupting the balance.

As the preparations continued, the signs of the ancient evil's awakening became more pronounced. The skies over the northern mountains grew darker, filled with ominous clouds that blocked out the sun. The earth trembled with increasing frequency, as if the very land itself was reacting to the presence of the darkness. Strange creatures, twisted and corrupted by the evil's influence, began to appear in the forests and valleys, their once peaceful natures turned to aggression and malice.

The people of the northern villages, though frightened by the growing darkness, remained steadfast in their resolve, bolstered by the presence of the fire giants and the dragons. They knew that their king and his council were doing everything in their power to protect them, and they placed their trust in the Phoenix King's leadership.

Finally, the day came when the Phoenix King and the council knew that they could wait no longer. The signs of the ancient evil's awakening were clear, and they could feel its influence spreading through the land like a dark cloud. The time had come to confront the evil directly, to face it in battle and put an end to its threat once and for all.

The Phoenix King, dressed in his battle armor and wielding the Staff of Renewal, led the council to the northern mountains, where the heart of the darkness lay. The fire giants marched beside him, their massive forms radiating strength and power, while the fire dragons soared above, their wings casting shadows over the land.

As they approached the source of the darkness, the air grew thick with malevolent energy, the very essence of the ancient evil that had awakened. The ground beneath their feet was scorched and barren, the trees twisted and lifeless, as if the land itself had been drained of all vitality.

The Phoenix King could feel the evil's presence growing stronger with each step, its influence pressing down on him like a heavy weight. But he did not falter, his heart filled with resolve as he led the council toward the center of the darkness.

Finally, they reached a vast, desolate valley, where the ground was blackened and cracked, and the air was filled with the stench of decay. At the center of the valley stood a massive, ancient structure—a fortress of dark stone, its walls covered in twisted, malevolent runes. This was the heart of the ancient evil, the place where it had lain dormant for centuries, waiting for the moment when it could awaken and spread its corruption across the land.

The Phoenix King raised the Staff of Renewal, its light cutting through the darkness like a beacon of hope. "This is where we make our stand," he said, his voice filled with determination. "The ancient evil has awakened, and it seeks to spread its corruption across our world. But we will not allow that to happen. We will confront this evil, and we will end its threat once and for all."

The fire giant leader stepped forward, his massive form towering over the others. "We are with you, Phoenix King," he rumbled, his voice filled with resolve. "We will fight this evil with all our strength, and we will protect our kingdom."

The elder fire dragon, his voice filled with ancient wisdom, added his support. "This evil has no place in our world. We will face it together, and we will ensure that the balance is maintained."

With the council united in purpose, the Phoenix King led the charge into the valley, the light of the Staff of Renewal guiding their way. The air was thick with the presence of the ancient evil, a malevolent force that seemed to twist and corrupt everything it touched. But the Phoenix King and the council pressed on, their resolve unshaken as they approached the dark fortress.

As they neared the fortress, the ground beneath their feet began to tremble, and the air was filled with a deafening roar. The ancient evil, sensing the presence of the Phoenix King and his council, unleashed its full power, summoning twisted, corrupted creatures from the depths of the earth to defend its stronghold.

The fire giants and dragons met the onslaught with fierce determination, their strength and elemental power cutting through the ranks of the corrupted creatures. The battle was intense, the air filled with the sound of clashing steel, roaring flames, and the cries of the fallen.

The Phoenix King, wielding the Staff of Renewal, fought at the forefront of the battle, his heart filled with resolve as he confronted the ancient evil. He could feel its malevolent energy pressing down on him, seeking to corrupt and twist his very soul, but he resisted with all his might, drawing upon the lessons he had learned and the power of the Eternal Flame.

As the battle raged on, the Phoenix King and the council fought their way through the ranks of the corrupted creatures, their goal clear—to reach the heart of the ancient evil and put an end to its threat once and for all.

Finally, after what felt like an eternity, the Phoenix King and the council reached the entrance to the dark fortress. The massive doors, covered in twisted runes, loomed before them, radiating a palpable sense of dread. The Phoenix King knew that beyond those doors lay the true heart of the ancient evil—the source of its power and corruption.

With a deep breath, the Phoenix King raised the Staff of Renewal, its light cutting through the darkness as he approached the doors. He could feel the ancient evil's presence growing stronger, its malevolent energy pressing down on him like a heavy weight. But he did not falter, his heart filled with resolve as he prepared to face the final challenge.

With a powerful surge of energy, the Phoenix King thrust the Staff of Renewal into the ground, its light spreading out in a brilliant wave that shattered the dark runes and forced the doors open with a deafening roar. The ground beneath their feet trembled, and the air was filled with a malevolent energy as the Phoenix King and the council stepped into the heart of the fortress.

The Final Confrontation

The interior of the fortress was a place of darkness and despair, its walls covered in twisted, malevolent runes that seemed to pulse with the energy of the ancient evil. The air was thick with the stench of decay, and the ground beneath their feet was blackened and cracked, as if the very essence of life had been drained from the land.

At the center of the fortress stood a massive, twisted throne, upon which sat the embodiment of the ancient evil—a being of pure darkness, its form shifting and writhing as if it were made of shadows and smoke. Its eyes, glowing with a malevolent light, fixed upon the Phoenix King and the council as they approached.

The Phoenix King could feel the ancient evil's power radiating from the throne, a force of corruption and destruction that sought to unravel the very fabric of reality. But he did not falter, his heart filled with resolve as he raised the Staff of Renewal, its light cutting through the darkness like a beacon of hope.

The ancient evil let out a deafening roar, its voice filled with malice and hatred. "You dare to challenge me, Phoenix King?" it hissed, its voice echoing through the fortress. "You are nothing but a fool, clinging to the weak notions of balance and renewal. I am the embodiment of darkness and destruction, and I will not be defeated by the likes of you."

The Phoenix King met the ancient evil's gaze, his voice strong and steady as he replied. "You are wrong. True power lies not in darkness and destruction, but in the balance between light and shadow, creation and destruction. I will not allow you to corrupt and twist our world. I will end your threat, and I will protect the balance."

With those words, the Phoenix King unleashed the full power of the Staff of Renewal, its light filling the fortress with a brilliant, radiant energy. The ancient evil let out a scream of fury as the light washed over it, its form writhing and twisting as it struggled to resist the purifying energy of the Eternal Flame.

The fire giants and dragons joined the battle, their strength and elemental power adding to the Phoenix King's assault. The air was filled with the sound of roaring flames and clashing steel as the council fought to subdue the ancient evil and cleanse the fortress of its malevolent influence.

The battle was intense, the ancient evil's power seemingly limitless as it fought to maintain its hold on the fortress. But the Phoenix King and the council fought with unwavering determination, their resolve unshaken as they pressed the attack.

Finally, after what felt like an eternity, the Phoenix King unleashed one final, powerful surge of energy from the Staff of Renewal, its light cutting through the darkness and striking at the heart of the ancient evil. The fortress trembled, and the air was filled with a deafening roar as the ancient evil let out a final scream of fury before its form disintegrated, consumed by the purifying light of the Eternal Flame.

As the ancient evil was vanquished, the darkness that had filled the fortress began to lift, replaced by a warm, radiant light. The twisted runes that had covered the walls faded away, and the ground beneath their feet began to heal, the blackened stone giving way to fresh, green earth.

The Phoenix King and the council stood in the center of the fortress, their hearts filled with relief and triumph as they realized that they had succeeded. The ancient evil had been defeated, and the balance of the world had been restored.

The fire giant leader, his voice filled with pride, spoke for the council. "We have done it, Phoenix King. The ancient evil is no more, and our world is safe once again."

The elder fire dragon, his voice filled with ancient wisdom, added his support. "The balance has been restored, and the cycles of life and death, creation and destruction, continue in harmony. This victory is a testament to the strength and wisdom of the Phoenix King and his council."

The Phoenix King, his heart filled with gratitude and resolve, nodded in agreement. "Thank you, my friends. We have faced a great challenge, and we have overcome it through our strength, our wisdom, and our unity. Together, we will continue to protect our kingdom and ensure that the balance of our world is maintained."

With those words, the Phoenix King and the council left the fortress, their hearts filled with a sense of accomplishment and purpose. They knew that there would be more challenges ahead, but they were ready to face them, knowing that they had the strength and wisdom to protect the balance and ensure the continued prosperity of the Phoenix Kingdom.

A New Beginning

The return to the Phoenix Kingdom was a triumphant one, the people of the kingdom celebrating the defeat of the ancient evil and the restoration of the balance. The Phoenix King and the Council of the Flames were hailed as heroes, their names becoming legends that would be passed down through generations.

The kingdom, once threatened by the darkness, now flourished with new life. The land, healed by the purifying light of the Eternal Flame, blossomed with vibrant colors and fresh growth. The rivers ran clear, the forests were filled with the sound of birdsong, and the people of the Phoenix Kingdom lived in peace and prosperity.

The Council of the Flames continued to meet regularly, guiding the kingdom with wisdom and strength. The fire giants and dragons remained steadfast allies, their knowledge and power ensuring that the balance of the world was maintained. The Phoenix King, ever mindful of the lessons he had learned, led his people with compassion and resolve, always seeking to protect the harmony of the world.

And so, the Phoenix King's reign continued, marked by peace, prosperity, and the delicate balance that held the world of Eldoria together. The Council of the Flames became a symbol of unity and strength, a testament to the power of collaboration and the importance of protecting the balance.

The legend of the Phoenix King and his council would be remembered for generations, their names becoming synonymous with hope, renewal, and the delicate balance that held the world of Eldoria together. The Phoenix King had risen to power, not just as a ruler, but as a guardian of the balance, a force for good in a world that had been forever changed by the flames of renewal.

And as the Phoenix King looked out over his kingdom, the flames of the Eternal Flame burning brightly in the distance, he knew that he was ready to lead his people into a future filled with hope, promise, and endless possibilities.

Chapter 12: The Shadow of Despair

The Birth of the Dark Phoenix

The victory over the ancient evil had brought a sense of peace and accomplishment to the Phoenix Kingdom. The people celebrated their king and the Council of the Flames, rejoicing in the restoration of balance and the promise of prosperity. The land, once threatened by darkness, had blossomed anew, and life flourished under the watchful eyes of the Phoenix King and his council.

Yet, in the depths of the earth, where the remnants of the ancient evil still lingered, something dark and malevolent was stirring. The forces of hatred and despair, though defeated, had not been entirely vanquished. Instead, they had gathered in the shadows, coalescing into a new form—a being born from the ashes of destruction, fueled by the very emotions that had given rise to the ancient evil.

This being, a twisted reflection of the Phoenix King, took the form of a dark phoenix, its body composed of black flames and smoldering embers. It was a creature of pure darkness, born from the remnants of the ancient evil and the hatred that had festered in the hearts of those it had touched. This dark phoenix, a shadow of despair, represented the destructive side of the Phoenix King's own power—a force that threatened to upset the delicate balance he had worked so hard to achieve.

The dark phoenix emerged from the depths of the earth, its wings unfurling in a storm of black fire. Its eyes, glowing with a malevolent light, surveyed the world with a hunger for destruction. It was a being of pure chaos, driven by a desire to unravel the balance and consume everything in its path.

As the dark phoenix rose into the sky, the land beneath it withered and died, the once vibrant fields turning to ash and dust. The skies darkened, filled with storm clouds that blotted out the sun, and the air grew thick with the stench of decay. The presence of the dark phoenix spread like a plague, corrupting everything it touched and leaving a trail of devastation in its wake.

The people of the Phoenix Kingdom, who had just begun to rebuild their lives after the defeat of the ancient evil, were once again plunged into fear and despair. The news of the dark phoenix's emergence spread quickly, and whispers of a new threat began to circulate throughout the kingdom. The celebrations of victory were cut short, replaced by a growing sense of dread as the shadow of despair loomed over the land.

The Phoenix King, who had been overseeing the restoration of the kingdom, was immediately alerted to the presence of the dark phoenix. He could feel its malevolent energy, a dark echo of his own power, and he knew that this was a threat unlike any he had faced before. The dark phoenix was not just an enemy—it was a manifestation of the destructive side of his own power, a force that threatened to consume him and everything he held dear.

With a heavy heart, the Phoenix King called an emergency meeting of the Council of the Flames. The members of the council, who had fought alongside him to defeat the ancient evil, gathered once more in the grand chamber, their expressions grim as they prepared to discuss this new and terrible threat.

The Council's Dilemma

The grand chamber, where the Council of the Flames met, was filled with a heavy atmosphere of concern and unease. The fire giants and dragons, who had been instrumental in the battle against the ancient evil, now faced a threat that was deeply personal to the Phoenix King and, by extension, to the balance they had all fought to protect.

The Phoenix King stood at the head of the table, his expression somber as he addressed the council. The Staff of Renewal, which had once shone with the light of hope and renewal, now seemed to carry the weight of the dark phoenix's presence, its light dimmed by the shadow of despair that had begun to spread across the land.

"My friends," the Phoenix King began, his voice heavy with the burden of responsibility. "We have faced many challenges together, and we have always emerged victorious through our strength, wisdom, and unity. But now we face a new threat—one that is born from the very power I wield."

The fire giant leader, a figure of immense strength and experience, nodded gravely. "Phoenix King, we have heard the reports of this dark phoenix, this creature of shadow and despair. It is clear that it poses a great threat to our kingdom, but it is also clear that this is no ordinary enemy. This creature is a part of you, born from the ashes of your own power. How can we hope to defeat it?"

The elder fire dragon, whose ancient wisdom had guided the council through many trials, spoke next, his voice filled with concern. "The dark phoenix is a manifestation of the destructive side of your power, Phoenix King. It is a being of chaos and hatred, driven by the same forces that gave rise to the ancient evil. To confront it is to confront a part of yourself, a part that has been twisted and corrupted by despair. This will not be an easy battle, and it may require sacrifices we have not yet considered."

The Phoenix King listened to the words of his council, his heart heavy with the knowledge that they spoke the truth. The dark phoenix was not just an external threat—it was a reflection of his own power, a force that had been born from the same flames that had given him life. To confront it would be to confront his own darkest impulses, the very aspects of his power that he had always sought to control and balance.

One of the scholars, a wise elder who had spent years studying the ancient texts, spoke up, his voice filled with urgency. "Phoenix King, there are legends of beings like the dark phoenix—creatures of shadow and flame that embody the destructive side of the elemental forces. These legends speak of the need to balance these forces, to confront and integrate the darkness within oneself in order to achieve true mastery. If the dark phoenix is a manifestation of your own power, then you must find a way to confront it without losing yourself to the darkness."

The Phoenix King nodded, his mind racing as he considered the implications of the scholar's words. He knew that the dark phoenix could not be defeated through sheer force alone—doing so would only strengthen the destructive side of his power, risking further imbalance. Instead, he would need to confront the dark phoenix in a way that acknowledged its existence while striving to restore the balance that had been disrupted.

The fire giant leader, his expression resolute, spoke for the council. "Phoenix King, we stand with you. Whatever course of action you choose, we will support you. We have fought alongside you before, and we will do so again. Together, we will find a way to restore the balance and protect our kingdom."

The elder fire dragon, his voice filled with ancient wisdom, added his support. "The dark phoenix is a formidable foe, but it is not invincible. We must approach this challenge with caution and care, but also with the determination to see it through to the end. The balance must be preserved, and we will do whatever it takes to ensure that it is."

The Phoenix King looked around the table, his gaze meeting that of each council member. Their support and resolve strengthened his own determination, and he knew that he could not face this challenge alone. The council had always been a source of strength and wisdom, and together, they would confront the shadow of despair that threatened their world.

"Thank you, my friends," the Phoenix King said, his voice filled with resolve. "We will face this challenge together, and we will find a way to restore the balance. The dark phoenix is a part of me, but it is also a threat to everything we have worked to achieve. I will confront it, and I will do so with the knowledge and strength that you have given me."

With those words, the council began to plan their strategy for confronting the dark phoenix. They knew that this would be a battle unlike any they had faced before—a battle not just against an external enemy, but against the very forces of darkness and despair that resided within the Phoenix King himself.

The Confrontation

The Phoenix King and the Council of the Flames prepared for the confrontation with the dark phoenix with a sense of urgency and determination. The reports from across the kingdom grew increasingly dire—the dark phoenix was spreading its influence, leaving a trail of devastation in its wake. The land, once vibrant and full of life, was withering under the shadow of despair, and the people were losing hope.

The Phoenix King knew that time was running out. The dark phoenix's presence was growing stronger with each passing day, and its malevolent energy was beginning to affect the balance of the world. The once harmonious cycles of life and death, creation and destruction, were becoming distorted, and the very fabric of reality seemed to be unraveling.

The council gathered in the grand chamber for what would likely be their final meeting before the confrontation. The mood was somber, the weight of the impending battle pressing down on them like a heavy shroud.

The Phoenix King, dressed in his battle armor and wielding the Staff of Renewal, addressed the council, his voice filled with resolve. "My friends, the time has come to confront the dark phoenix. This creature of shadow and despair has already caused great harm to our kingdom, and it threatens to destroy everything we have worked to protect. We must face it now, before its influence spreads any further."

The fire giant leader, his expression grim, nodded in agreement. "Phoenix King, we are ready. The fire giants will stand by your side in battle, and we will do whatever it takes to protect our kingdom and restore the balance."

The elder fire dragon, his voice filled with ancient wisdom, added his support. "The dark phoenix is a formidable foe, but it is not invincible. We must approach this battle with caution and care, but also with the determination to see it through to the end. The balance must be preserved, and we will do whatever it takes to ensure that it is."

The Phoenix King nodded, his heart filled with gratitude for the unwavering support of his council. "Thank you, my friends," he said. "Together, we will face the dark phoenix and restore the balance. But remember, this battle will not be won through sheer force alone. We must find a way to confront the darkness without losing ourselves to it. The balance must be maintained, even as we fight to protect it."

With the council's plan in place, the Phoenix King and his allies prepared to confront the dark phoenix. They knew that the battle ahead would be difficult, but they were determined to see it through. The fate of the kingdom—and the balance of the world—depended on their success.

The Phoenix King led the council to the heart of the dark phoenix's influence—a desolate wasteland where the land had been scorched and twisted by the creature's malevolent energy. The skies above were dark and stormy, filled with swirling clouds of ash and smoke. The air was thick with the stench of decay, and the ground beneath their feet was blackened and cracked, as if the very essence of life had been drained from the earth.

As they approached the center of the wasteland, the dark phoenix appeared, its massive form looming over the desolate landscape. The creature's body was composed of black flames and smoldering embers, its wings spreading wide as it let out a deafening screech that echoed across the land. Its eyes, glowing with a malevolent light, fixed upon the Phoenix King and his allies, radiating hatred and despair.

The Phoenix King could feel the dark phoenix's presence pressing down on him like a heavy weight, its malevolent energy seeking to corrupt and twist his very soul. But he did not falter, his heart filled with resolve as he raised the Staff of Renewal, its light cutting through the darkness like a beacon of hope.

The dark phoenix let out another screech, its voice filled with malice and hatred. "You dare to challenge me, Phoenix King?" it hissed, its voice echoing through the wasteland. "I am the shadow of your own power, born from the ashes of your hatred and despair. You cannot defeat me, for I am a part of you."

The Phoenix King met the dark phoenix's gaze, his voice strong and steady as he replied. "You are wrong. You are a twisted reflection of my power, a manifestation of the darkness within me. But I am not defined by that darkness. I am the Phoenix King, and I will not allow you to corrupt and destroy everything I hold dear."

With those words, the Phoenix King unleashed the full power of the Staff of Renewal, its light filling the wasteland with a brilliant, radiant energy. The dark phoenix let out a screech of fury as the light washed over it, its form writhing and twisting as it struggled to resist the purifying energy of the Eternal Flame.

The fire giants and dragons joined the battle, their strength and elemental power adding to the Phoenix King's assault. The air was filled with the sound of roaring flames and clashing forces as the council fought to subdue the dark phoenix and cleanse the land of its malevolent influence.

The battle was intense, the dark phoenix's power seemingly limitless as it fought to maintain its hold on the wasteland. But the Phoenix King and the council fought with unwavering determination, their resolve unshaken as they pressed the attack.

As the battle raged on, the Phoenix King realized that defeating the dark phoenix would require more than just strength and power. He could feel the creature's connection to his own power, a dark echo of the flames that burned within him. To truly defeat the dark phoenix, he would need to confront the darkness within himself, to acknowledge the destructive side of his power and find a way to integrate it without losing himself to it.

The Phoenix King took a deep breath, his heart filled with resolve as he lowered the Staff of Renewal. He knew that the time had come to confront the dark phoenix not as an enemy, but as a part of himself—a part that he needed to understand and integrate in order to restore the balance.

With the battle still raging around him, the Phoenix King stepped forward, his voice calm and steady as he addressed the dark phoenix. "You are a part of me," he said, his voice filled with understanding. "You are the shadow of my own power, born from the darkness within me. But you do not define me. I am the Phoenix King, and I choose to embrace the light as well as the darkness. Together, we can restore the balance."

The dark phoenix let out a screech of fury, its form writhing as it struggled to resist the Phoenix King's words. But the Phoenix King did not falter, his heart filled with compassion as he reached out to the creature with the light of the Eternal Flame.

The light of the Staff of Renewal flared to life, filling the wasteland with a brilliant, radiant energy that cut through the darkness like a beacon of hope. The dark phoenix let out a final screech as the light washed over it, its form dissolving into a storm of black flames and smoldering embers.

As the dark phoenix disintegrated, the wasteland began to heal, the blackened earth giving way to fresh, green growth. The skies cleared, the storm clouds dissipating as the light of the Eternal Flame spread across the land.

The Phoenix King stood in the center of the wasteland, his heart filled with a sense of accomplishment and understanding. He had confronted the darkness within himself, and in doing so, he had restored the balance and protected his kingdom from the shadow of despair.

The fire giants and dragons, their expressions filled with relief and admiration, approached the Phoenix King, their voices filled with praise and respect. "You have done it, Phoenix King," the fire giant leader said, his voice filled with pride. "You have defeated the dark phoenix and restored the balance. We are honored to have fought alongside you."

The elder fire dragon, his voice filled with ancient wisdom, added his support. "You have shown great strength and wisdom, Phoenix King. By confronting the darkness within yourself, you have ensured that the balance of our world is maintained. The kingdom is safe once again."

The Phoenix King nodded, his heart filled with gratitude for the unwavering support of his council. "Thank you, my friends," he said. "We have faced a great challenge, and we have overcome it together. The dark phoenix was a formidable foe, but it has been defeated. The balance is restored, and our kingdom is safe."

The Aftermath

The return to the Phoenix Kingdom was a triumphant one, the people celebrating the defeat of the dark phoenix and the restoration of balance. The land, once threatened by the shadow of despair, now flourished with new life. The skies were clear, the rivers ran fresh, and the fields yielded abundant harvests.

The Phoenix King, ever mindful of the lessons he had learned, continued to lead his people with compassion and resolve. He understood now more than ever that true power lay not in the denial of darkness, but in the balance between light and shadow, creation and destruction. He knew that the darkness within himself was a part of his power, but it did not define him.

The Council of the Flames continued to guide the kingdom with wisdom and strength, their unity and resolve ensuring that the balance was maintained. The fire giants and dragons remained steadfast allies, their knowledge and power contributing to the continued prosperity of the Phoenix Kingdom.

The legend of the Phoenix King and his battle against the dark phoenix became a symbol of hope and renewal, a testament to the power of confronting and integrating the darkness within oneself. The people of the Phoenix Kingdom looked to their king with pride and admiration, knowing that they were in the hands of a ruler who would protect the balance and lead them into a future filled with promise and possibility.

And so, the Phoenix King's reign continued, marked by peace, prosperity, and the delicate balance that held the world of Eldoria together. The shadow of despair had been vanquished, and the light of the Eternal Flame burned brighter than ever, guiding the kingdom toward a future of hope and renewal.

The Phoenix King had risen to power, not just as a ruler, but as a guardian of the balance, a force for good in a world that had been forever changed by the flames of renewal. And as he looked out over his kingdom, the flames of the Eternal Flame burning brightly in the distance, he knew that he was ready to lead his people into a future filled with endless possibilities.

Chapter 13: The Battle of the Two Flames

The Gathering Storm

The Phoenix Kingdom had experienced a period of relative peace after the confrontation with the dark phoenix, but the shadow of despair still lingered in the hearts of the people. The dark phoenix, though seemingly defeated, had left its mark on the land—a reminder that the forces of creation and destruction were not so easily separated. The Phoenix King knew that the final battle with his dark counterpart was inevitable, and it would determine the fate of his kingdom.

In the days leading up to the battle, the skies above the Phoenix Kingdom began to change. Dark clouds gathered on the horizon, swirling with ominous energy. The air was thick with tension, as if the very elements themselves were preparing for the clash of two powerful forces. The people of the kingdom sensed the impending conflict, and fear spread through the land like wildfire.

The Phoenix King, ever vigilant, knew that the time had come to confront the dark phoenix once and for all. The creature had not been fully vanquished; instead, it had retreated to the depths of the earth, where it had been gathering strength. Now, it was ready to rise again, and this time, it would stop at nothing to assert its dominance over the Phoenix Kingdom.

The Council of the Flames convened one last time before the battle. The grand chamber, usually filled with the warm light of the Eternal Flame, was now dimly lit, the flames flickering uneasily as if reflecting the uncertainty that hung in the air.

The Phoenix King stood at the head of the table, his expression resolute but tinged with the weight of the decision he knew he would soon have to make. The Staff of Renewal, which had guided him through many trials, now felt heavier in his grasp—a symbol of the choices that lay ahead.

"My friends," the Phoenix King began, his voice steady but somber, "the time has come to face the dark phoenix once more. This creature is not just an enemy; it is a reflection of my own power, a manifestation of the destructive forces that reside within me. We have fought many battles together, but this one will be different. The fate of our kingdom—and the balance of the world—depends on the outcome of this battle."

The fire giant leader, a figure of immense strength and experience, nodded gravely. "Phoenix King, we stand with you. The dark phoenix is a formidable foe, but we have faced great challenges before, and we have overcome them. We will do whatever it takes to protect our kingdom."

The elder fire dragon, whose wisdom had guided the council through countless trials, spoke next, his voice filled with concern. "This battle will not be won through force alone, Phoenix King. The dark phoenix is a part of you, a force that embodies the destructive side of your power. You must find a way to confront it without losing yourself to the darkness. The balance must be maintained, even in the midst of battle."

The Phoenix King listened to the counsel of his allies, his heart heavy with the knowledge that they spoke the truth. The battle ahead would not be a simple clash of forces; it would be a test of his ability to balance the light and dark within himself. He would need to confront the dark phoenix not just as an enemy, but as a part of his own being—a part that he needed to understand and integrate in order to achieve true mastery over his power.

The scholar, who had studied the ancient texts and legends of the Phoenix Kingdom, spoke up, his voice filled with urgency. "Phoenix King, there are ancient prophecies that speak of this battle—a battle between two flames, where the forces of creation and destruction collide. The prophecies suggest that the outcome of this battle will determine the fate of our world. You must choose wisely, for the choice you make will have far-reaching consequences."

The Phoenix King nodded, his mind racing as he considered the implications of the scholar's words. He knew that the battle ahead would be difficult, but he also knew that the outcome would depend not just on his strength, but on his ability to make the right choice—a choice that would determine the future of the Phoenix Kingdom and the balance of the world.

"Thank you, my friends," the Phoenix King said, his voice filled with resolve. "We have faced many challenges together, and we have always emerged stronger. This battle will be our greatest test, but I believe that we can overcome it. I will confront the dark phoenix, and I will do so with the knowledge and strength that you have given me."

With those words, the council dispersed, each member preparing in their own way for the battle that was to come. The Phoenix King, however, remained in the grand chamber, his heart heavy with the weight of the decision he knew he would soon have to make. The choice before him was clear: to destroy the dark phoenix and risk upsetting the balance, or to find a way to integrate the two forces, ensuring that the light and dark within him remained in harmony.

The Battle Begins

The day of the battle dawned with a sky filled with swirling clouds of dark and light, a visual manifestation of the clash of forces that was about to take place. The Phoenix King, dressed in his battle armor and wielding the Staff of Renewal, stood at the edge of a cliff overlooking the kingdom, his gaze fixed on the horizon where the dark phoenix would soon appear.

The Council of the Flames stood behind him, their expressions grim but resolute. The fire giants, their bodies radiating strength and power, were ready to defend the kingdom, while the fire dragons, their wings spread wide, prepared to take to the skies in support of their king.

As the sun reached its zenith, the dark phoenix emerged from the depths of the earth, its massive form rising into the sky like a storm of black flames. The creature's wings unfurled, casting a shadow over the land as it let out a deafening screech that echoed across the kingdom. Its eyes, glowing with a malevolent light, fixed upon the Phoenix King, radiating hatred and despair.

The Phoenix King could feel the dark phoenix's presence pressing down on him like a heavy weight, its malevolent energy seeking to corrupt and twist his very soul. But he did not falter, his heart filled with resolve as he raised the Staff of Renewal, its light cutting through the darkness like a beacon of hope.

The dark phoenix let out another screech, its voice filled with malice and hatred. "Phoenix King, you cannot defeat me," it hissed, its voice echoing through the skies. "I am the shadow of your own power, born from the ashes of your hatred and despair. You cannot destroy me, for I am a part of you."

The Phoenix King met the dark phoenix's gaze, his voice strong and steady as he replied. "You are a part of me, but you do not define me. I am the Phoenix King, and I choose to embrace both the light and the darkness within me. Together, we can restore the balance and protect our kingdom."

With those words, the Phoenix King took to the skies, his wings ablaze with the radiant flames of the Eternal Flame. The dark phoenix rose to meet him, its wings spreading wide as it unleashed a torrent of black fire. The two forces collided in a brilliant explosion of light and dark, their powers clashing with a force that shook the very heavens.

The battle between the two flames was fierce and unrelenting, each strike and counterstrike sending shockwaves through the air. The skies above the Phoenix Kingdom were filled with the sound of roaring flames and clashing forces as the Phoenix King and the dark phoenix fought for dominance.

The Phoenix King wielded the Staff of Renewal with precision and control, using its power to counter the dark phoenix's attacks and protect the kingdom below. But he could feel the strain of the battle, the dark phoenix's malevolent energy pressing down on him like a crushing weight. It was as if the creature was trying to draw out the darkness within him, to corrupt and twist his power until it was indistinguishable from its own.

The Phoenix King knew that he could not allow the dark phoenix to succeed. He had to find a way to confront the creature without losing himself to the darkness, to restore the balance without destroying the very forces that made him who he was.

As the battle raged on, the Phoenix King realized that the key to defeating the dark phoenix lay not in destroying it, but in understanding it. The creature was a manifestation of his own power, a reflection of the destructive forces that resided within him. To truly defeat the dark phoenix, he would need to confront the darkness within himself and find a way to integrate the two forces, ensuring that the light and dark within him remained in harmony.

With this realization, the Phoenix King began to change his approach. Instead of attacking the dark phoenix with brute force, he began to use the Staff of Renewal to channel his own energy into the creature, seeking to understand its nature and find a way to bring it into balance with the light.

The dark phoenix, sensing the change in the Phoenix King's tactics, let out a screech of fury, its form writhing and twisting as it struggled to resist the purifying energy of the Eternal Flame. But the Phoenix King did not relent, his heart filled with resolve as he continued to channel his energy into the creature, seeking to integrate the two forces within himself.

The Choice

The battle between the two flames reached its climax, the skies above the Phoenix Kingdom filled with a brilliant, radiant light as the Phoenix King and the dark phoenix clashed one final time. The air was thick with energy, the very fabric of reality trembling as the forces of creation and destruction collided in a final, decisive moment.

The Phoenix King, his heart heavy with the weight of the decision he knew he had to make, faced the dark phoenix one last time. The creature, its form flickering with the energy of the Eternal Flame, let out a final screech as it realized that its fate was in the Phoenix King's hands.

The Phoenix King knew that he had two choices: to destroy the dark phoenix and risk upsetting the balance, or to find a way to integrate the two forces, ensuring that the light and dark within him remained in harmony. It was a choice that would determine the future of the Phoenix Kingdom and the balance of the world.

The dark phoenix, its voice filled with desperation, hissed at the Phoenix King. "You cannot destroy me," it whispered, its voice echoing through the air. "I am a part of you, a force that has always been within you. If you destroy me, you will destroy a part of yourself."

The Phoenix King, his heart filled with compassion and understanding, knew that the dark phoenix spoke the truth. The creature was a part of him, a manifestation of the destructive forces that resided within him. To destroy it would be to deny a part of himself, to upset the balance that he had worked so hard to maintain.

With a deep breath, the Phoenix King made his choice. He would not destroy the dark phoenix; instead, he would seek to integrate it, to bring the forces of light and dark within himself into harmony.

Raising the Staff of Renewal, the Phoenix King channeled his energy into the dark phoenix, seeking to understand its nature and bring it into balance with the light. The creature, sensing the Phoenix King's intent, let out a final, agonized screech as its form began to change, the black flames of its body merging with the radiant light of the Eternal Flame.

The process was intense and painful, the air filled with the sound of crackling flames and the roar of energy as the Phoenix King and the dark phoenix became one. The skies above the Phoenix Kingdom were filled with a brilliant, radiant light, the very essence of creation and destruction merging into a single, harmonious force.

The Phoenix King could feel the darkness within himself being transformed, the destructive forces that had once threatened to consume him now integrated into his being. The light and dark within him were no longer in conflict; instead, they existed in perfect balance, each one complementing the other.

As the transformation reached its climax, the dark phoenix let out a final, echoing screech before its form dissolved into a storm of radiant light and black flames. The energy of the Eternal Flame surged through the Phoenix King, filling him with a sense of completion and understanding.

The battle was over. The dark phoenix was no more, and the Phoenix King had emerged victorious—not by destroying his dark counterpart, but by integrating it, ensuring that the forces of creation and destruction within him remained in perfect harmony.

The Aftermath

The skies above the Phoenix Kingdom began to clear, the dark clouds dissipating as the radiant light of the Eternal Flame spread across the land. The people of the kingdom, who had watched the battle unfold with fear and uncertainty, now rejoiced as they realized that their king had emerged victorious.

The Phoenix King, his heart filled with a sense of accomplishment and understanding, descended from the skies, the Staff of Renewal still glowing with the energy of the battle. He knew that the choice he had made would have far-reaching consequences, but he was confident that it was the right one.

The Council of the Flames, who had watched the battle from below, approached the Phoenix King, their expressions filled with relief and admiration. The fire giant leader, his voice filled with pride, spoke for the council. "Phoenix King, you have done it. You have faced the dark phoenix and emerged victorious. The balance has been restored, and our kingdom is safe once again."

The elder fire dragon, his voice filled with ancient wisdom, added his support. "You have shown great strength and wisdom, Phoenix King. By choosing to integrate the dark phoenix, you have ensured that the forces of light and dark within you remain in harmony. The balance of our world is maintained, and the future of our kingdom is secure."

The Phoenix King nodded, his heart filled with gratitude for the unwavering support of his council. "Thank you, my friends," he said. "This battle was not won through force alone, but through understanding and integration. The dark phoenix was a part of me, and by choosing to integrate it, I have ensured that the balance within me—and within our kingdom—remains intact."

The Council of the Flames, their hearts filled with admiration for their king, pledged their continued support and loyalty. They knew that the Phoenix King's reign would continue to be marked by peace, prosperity, and the delicate balance that held the world of Eldoria together.

The legend of the Battle of the Two Flames became a symbol of hope and renewal, a testament to the power of understanding and integration. The people of the Phoenix Kingdom looked to their king with pride and admiration, knowing that they were in the hands of a ruler who would protect the balance and lead them into a future filled with promise and possibility.

And so, the Phoenix King's reign continued, marked by peace, prosperity, and the delicate balance that held the world of Eldoria together. The forces of creation and destruction, light and dark, existed in harmony within the Phoenix King, ensuring that the kingdom remained strong and prosperous.

The Phoenix King had risen to power, not just as a ruler, but as a guardian of the balance, a force for good in a world that had been forever changed by the flames of renewal. And as he looked out over his kingdom, the flames of the Eternal Flame burning brightly in the distance, he knew that he was ready to lead his people into a future filled with endless possibilities.

Chapter 14: The Balance Restored

The Moment of Unity

The skies above the Phoenix Kingdom were serene once more, their tranquil blue a stark contrast to the tumultuous storm that had raged during the battle between the Phoenix King and the dark phoenix. The battle had been a fierce contest of wills, power, and existential reckoning, and the outcome had changed everything. Where there had once been two opposing forces—light and dark, creation and destruction—there was now a single, harmonious entity. The Phoenix King had chosen unity over destruction, merging with the dark phoenix to create a new, balanced being.

This act was not one of simple conquest; it was a deliberate choice to embrace all aspects of his nature. The Phoenix King knew that to deny the darkness would be to deny a part of himself, a part that was as vital to the balance as the light. By integrating the dark phoenix, he had not only defeated a formidable foe but had also transcended the limitations of his former self. The new entity that emerged from this union was more powerful, more complete, and wiser in ways that the Phoenix King could not have anticipated.

As the dust settled and the skies cleared, the Phoenix Kingdom began to feel the effects of this profound transformation. The land itself seemed to respond to the change within its ruler. Where the ground had been scarred by the destructive forces of the battle, new life began to emerge. Flowers bloomed in vibrant colors, trees that had been charred by the dark phoenix's flames sprouted fresh, green leaves, and the rivers that had run dry during the conflict now flowed with crystal-clear water. The cycle of life and death, which had been thrown into disarray, was restored to its natural rhythm, and the kingdom flourished.

The people of the Phoenix Kingdom, who had watched the battle from afar with bated breath, now rejoiced as they witnessed the renewal of their land. The fear and uncertainty that had gripped their hearts during the battle gave way to hope and optimism. They knew that their king had not only protected them from a great threat but had also ushered in a new era—one of balance, peace, and prosperity.

The Council of the Flames, who had been steadfast in their support of the Phoenix King, gathered once more in the grand chamber to discuss the implications of the recent events. The mood in the room was one of cautious optimism, tempered by the weight of the decisions that had been made. The Phoenix King, who now embodied both the light and the dark, sat at the head of the table, his presence more commanding than ever before.

The New Entity

The Phoenix King had undergone a profound transformation, both physically and spiritually. The merger with the dark phoenix had altered his appearance in subtle but significant ways. His once golden-red feathers, symbols of his royal lineage, now bore streaks of deep black, a visual reminder of the darkness he had embraced. His eyes, which had always burned with the intensity of the Eternal Flame, now held a depth that reflected the wisdom of ages and the understanding of both creation and destruction. The Staff of Renewal, which had been his trusted weapon and symbol of his rule, now glowed with a new, more complex energy—a blend of light and dark that represented the unity he had achieved.

As the council members took their seats, they could feel the change in their king. There was a new aura of power that surrounded him, one that was both awe-inspiring and humbling. The Phoenix King had always been a symbol of hope and renewal, but now he was something more—a being who had transcended the duality of existence to become a guardian of the balance itself.

The fire giant leader, whose loyalty and strength had been unwavering, was the first to speak. His deep, resonant voice filled the chamber, carrying with it the weight of centuries of wisdom. "Phoenix King, you have achieved something that few could even imagine. By merging with the dark phoenix, you have not only protected our kingdom but have also restored the balance of the world. We are in awe of your strength and wisdom."

The elder fire dragon, whose ancient knowledge had guided the council through many challenges, nodded in agreement. His voice, as ancient and enduring as the mountains themselves, was filled with reverence. "Phoenix King, your choice to embrace the darkness as a part of yourself has set a new precedent. You have shown us that true power lies not in the denial of our darker aspects but in their integration. This new entity you have become is a beacon of hope for all of Eldoria."

The Phoenix King listened to the words of his council, his heart filled with gratitude and humility. He knew that the choice he had made had been the right one, but he also understood that this was only the beginning. The balance had been restored, but it was now his responsibility to maintain it, to ensure that the forces of creation and destruction remained in harmony.

"Thank you, my friends," the Phoenix King said, his voice calm and steady, yet imbued with the new power he now possessed. "The battle with the dark phoenix was a test of not just my strength but my understanding of what it means to rule. I have learned that true power does not come from the ability to destroy or create alone, but from the ability to balance these forces within oneself. This new entity that I have become is a testament to that truth."

The scholar, whose knowledge of ancient texts had been invaluable, spoke next, his voice filled with curiosity and admiration. "Phoenix King, this new entity you have become is something that our legends have never foretold. You are now both the guardian of the light and the keeper of the darkness. How do you envision this will affect your rule and the future of our kingdom?"

The Phoenix King took a moment to consider the scholar's question. He knew that his transformation would have far-reaching implications, not just for his rule but for the entire kingdom and beyond. The integration of the dark phoenix had granted him new insights, new powers, but it had also placed upon him a greater responsibility—to maintain the delicate balance between life and death, creation and destruction.

"Our kingdom," the Phoenix King began, his voice filled with the wisdom of his new understanding, "has always been a place of renewal, a place where life is celebrated and protected. But we must also acknowledge that destruction is a part of the cycle of existence. The dark phoenix was a manifestation of that truth—a force that I had to confront and integrate in order to maintain the balance. Going forward, we will need to embrace this understanding as a kingdom. We will continue to protect life, but we will also respect the role that destruction plays in the cycle of renewal."

The council members nodded in agreement, their expressions reflecting their acceptance of this new reality. They understood that the Phoenix King's transformation marked the beginning of a new era—one where the forces of creation and destruction would be acknowledged and balanced, ensuring the continued prosperity of the kingdom.

The Restoration of Harmony

With the dark phoenix now integrated into the Phoenix King, the kingdom began to experience a profound renewal. The cycle of life and death, which had been disrupted by the battle, was now fully restored. The land, once scarred by the destructive forces unleashed during the conflict, was now flourishing with new life. The fields yielded abundant harvests, the forests were filled with the sounds of thriving wildlife, and the rivers ran clear and strong. It was as if the very essence of the kingdom had been revitalized by the Phoenix King's transformation.

The people of the Phoenix Kingdom, who had lived in fear and uncertainty during the battle, now rejoiced in the restoration of harmony. They could feel the change in the air, a palpable sense of balance that permeated every aspect of their lives. The Phoenix King's decision to embrace the dark phoenix had not only saved them from destruction but had also brought about a deeper understanding of the cycles that governed their world.

The Phoenix King, now more powerful and wise than ever before, took it upon himself to ensure that this newfound balance was maintained. He traveled throughout the kingdom, visiting the villages and towns that had been most affected by the battle. He spoke with the people, listening to their concerns and offering them reassurance. His presence, now imbued with the combined energies of creation and destruction, was a source of comfort and inspiration to all who encountered him.

In one such village, a place that had been on the front lines of the battle with the dark phoenix, the Phoenix King found himself speaking to a gathering of villagers who had lost their homes and livelihoods during the conflict. The people were weary and uncertain, but they were also filled with hope, knowing that their king had emerged victorious and that the balance had been restored.

One of the villagers, an elderly woman whose eyes bore the wisdom of many years, stepped forward to address the Phoenix King. "My lord," she said, her voice trembling with emotion, "we have lost much during this time of darkness. But we are grateful that you have brought us back into the light. How can we ever repay you for what you have done?"

The Phoenix King, his heart filled with compassion, knelt before the woman, taking her hands in his. "There is no need for repayment," he said gently. "The balance of our world is something that we must all work to maintain. What I have done, I have done for all of us—for the future of our kingdom. But know this: the strength to restore and renew does not lie with me alone. It lies within each of you. Together, we will rebuild what has been lost, and together, we will ensure that the balance is preserved."

The woman, her eyes brimming with tears, nodded in understanding. "Thank you, my lord," she whispered. "We will do our part."

The Phoenix King smiled, his heart filled with a sense of purpose. He knew that the restoration of harmony in the kingdom would require the efforts of all its people, and he was determined to lead them in this new era of peace and prosperity.

As the days turned into weeks and the weeks into months, the Phoenix Kingdom continued to flourish. The people, inspired by their king's example, worked tirelessly to rebuild their homes and restore their communities. The fields were once again filled with crops, the markets buzzed with activity, and the sounds of laughter and joy echoed through the streets. The dark days of the battle were behind them, and the future was filled with promise.

The Council of the Flames played a vital role in this restoration, offering their guidance and support to the Phoenix King as he navigated the challenges of this new era. The fire giants, with their immense strength, helped to rebuild the kingdom's infrastructure, while the fire dragons, with their ancient wisdom, offered counsel on matters of governance and strategy. The scholars, whose knowledge of the ancient texts had been invaluable, continued to study the implications of the Phoenix King's transformation, seeking to understand the deeper mysteries of the balance.

The Phoenix King, for his part, remained vigilant, always mindful of the delicate balance he had achieved. He knew that the forces of creation and destruction, though now in harmony, would always require careful management. The dark phoenix, now a part of him, served as a constant reminder of the power and responsibility he wielded. But he also knew that he was not alone in this task. The people of the Phoenix Kingdom, the Council of the Flames, and the very land itself were all part of the balance, and together, they would ensure its preservation.

A New Era of Peace and Prosperity

The Phoenix King's transformation marked the beginning of a new era for the Phoenix Kingdom—an era of peace, prosperity, and harmony. The integration of the dark phoenix had not only restored the balance but had also brought about a deeper understanding of the forces that governed their world. The people, who had once lived in fear of the destructive powers that threatened their land, now embraced the cycle of life and death, creation and destruction, as essential aspects of their existence.

The Phoenix King, now a being of both light and dark, ruled with wisdom and compassion. His decisions were guided by the understanding that true power lay not in the ability to create or destroy, but in the ability to balance these forces within oneself. He continued to travel throughout the kingdom, ensuring that the lessons of the past were not forgotten and that the people remained vigilant in their efforts to maintain the balance.

One of the key initiatives of this new era was the establishment of schools and academies throughout the kingdom, where the next generation could learn about the cycle of life and death and the importance of balance. These institutions, which were supported by the Council of the Flames, became centers of learning and innovation, attracting scholars and students from all corners of Eldoria. The Phoenix King himself often visited these schools, sharing his knowledge and experiences with the students and encouraging them to think critically about the world around them.

In one such visit, the Phoenix King found himself speaking to a group of young students who were eager to learn about the battle with the dark phoenix and the lessons it had taught. The students, their faces filled with curiosity and wonder, asked the Phoenix King about his transformation and what it meant for the future of the kingdom.

"Phoenix King," one of the students, a bright-eyed boy with a quick mind, asked, "how did you know that merging with the dark phoenix was the right choice? Weren't you afraid that it would make you too powerful or that it would change you in ways you couldn't control?"

The Phoenix King, his expression thoughtful, considered the boy's question before answering. "I was afraid," he admitted, his voice gentle yet firm. "The dark phoenix was a powerful force, one that could have easily consumed me if I had allowed it. But I also knew that to deny it would be to deny a part of myself—a part that was essential to the balance. The choice to merge with the dark phoenix was not an easy one, but it was the right one. It has taught me that true power comes from understanding and integrating all aspects of ourselves, even those that we may fear."

The students listened intently, their minds absorbing the wisdom of their king. They knew that they were witnessing something extraordinary—a leader who had faced his darkest fears and emerged stronger, wiser, and more complete. The Phoenix King's transformation was a lesson in humility, courage, and the importance of balance, and it was a lesson that would guide them throughout their lives.

As the years passed, the Phoenix Kingdom continued to thrive. The fields yielded bountiful harvests, the forests were lush and vibrant, and the people lived in peace and harmony. The cycle of life and death, creation and destruction, was acknowledged and respected, and the balance that had been restored by the Phoenix King's transformation remained intact.

The legend of the Phoenix King and the battle with the dark phoenix became a story that was told and retold throughout the kingdom—a story of courage, wisdom, and the power of unity. The people of the Phoenix Kingdom took pride in their king, knowing that they were part of something greater than themselves—a kingdom that was built on the principles of balance, renewal, and harmony.

And so, the Phoenix King's reign continued, marked by peace, prosperity, and the delicate balance that held the world of Eldoria together. The forces of creation and destruction, light and dark, existed in harmony within the Phoenix King, ensuring that the kingdom remained strong and prosperous.

The Phoenix King had risen to power, not just as a ruler, but as a guardian of the balance, a force for good in a world that had been forever changed by the flames of renewal. And as he looked out over his kingdom, the flames of the Eternal Flame burning brightly in the distance, he knew that he was ready to lead his people into a future filled with endless possibilities.

The Legacy of the Phoenix King

The legacy of the Phoenix King was one of wisdom, balance, and renewal. His decision to merge with the dark phoenix had not only saved his kingdom but had also set a new standard for leadership and governance. The people of the Phoenix Kingdom, inspired by their king's example, continued to embrace the principles of balance in their own lives, understanding that true strength came from the integration of all aspects of existence.

The Council of the Flames, which had supported the Phoenix King throughout his journey, remained a vital part of the kingdom's governance. The fire giants and dragons, with their immense strength and ancient wisdom, continued to play a crucial role in maintaining the balance, offering their guidance and support to the Phoenix King and his people. The scholars, whose knowledge of the ancient texts had been invaluable, continued to study and interpret the mysteries of the balance, ensuring that the lessons of the past were not forgotten.

The Phoenix King, now a being of both light and dark, ruled with a deep understanding of the forces that governed his world. He knew that the balance was a delicate thing, one that required constant vigilance and care. But he also knew that he was not alone in this task. The people of the Phoenix Kingdom, the Council of the Flames, and the very land itself were all part of the balance, and together, they would ensure its preservation.

As the years passed, the Phoenix King's influence extended beyond the borders of his kingdom. Other realms, witnessing the peace and prosperity that had come from the restoration of the balance, sought to learn from the Phoenix King's example. Diplomats and emissaries from distant lands traveled to the Phoenix Kingdom, seeking to understand the principles that had guided the Phoenix King in his decisions.

The Phoenix King, always mindful of his responsibility as a guardian of the balance, welcomed these visitors with open arms. He shared his knowledge and experiences with them, encouraging them to think critically about the forces that governed their own realms and to seek ways to integrate and balance those forces within their societies.

In time, the principles of balance and renewal that had been established in the Phoenix Kingdom began to spread throughout Eldoria. Other kingdoms, inspired by the Phoenix King's example, adopted similar practices, ensuring that the cycles of life and death, creation and destruction, were acknowledged and respected. The world of Eldoria, once fraught with conflict and instability, was now a place of harmony and balance, where the forces of light and dark coexisted in peace.

The Phoenix King's reign was remembered as a golden age—a time when the balance was restored, and the kingdom flourished. The people of the Phoenix Kingdom, who had once lived in fear of the destructive forces that threatened their land, now lived in peace and prosperity, secure in the knowledge that their king was a guardian of the balance.

And as the Phoenix King looked out over his kingdom, the flames of the Eternal Flame burning brightly in the distance, he knew that his journey was far from over. The balance, though restored, would always require careful management and vigilance. But with the wisdom and strength he had gained through his trials, he was ready to face whatever challenges lay ahead.

The Phoenix King had become more than just a ruler; he had become a symbol of hope, renewal, and the power of unity. His legacy would endure for generations, a testament to the strength of the human spirit and the importance of balance in a world that was constantly changing.

And so, the Phoenix King's story continued—a story of light and dark, creation and destruction, and the delicate balance that held the world of Eldoria together. A story that would inspire future generations to seek wisdom, to embrace all aspects of themselves, and to strive for a world where harmony and balance were the guiding principles.

The balance had been restored, and with it, a new era of peace and prosperity had begun. The Phoenix Kingdom, under the wise and compassionate rule of the Phoenix King, would continue to flourish, a shining example of what could be achieved when unity and understanding prevailed.

And as the Phoenix King looked out over his kingdom, the flames of the Eternal Flame burning brightly in the distance, he knew that the future was filled with endless possibilities. The balance was intact, and the world of Eldoria was at peace—a peace that would endure for generations to come.

Chapter 15: The Immortal Fire

The Final Reflections

The Phoenix Kingdom, nestled within the heart of Eldoria, had witnessed countless transformations over the ages. From the fires of creation to the shadows of despair, the kingdom had endured trials that tested the limits of its resilience. At the center of these trials was the Phoenix King, a figure of legend who had risen from the flames of both creation and destruction to lead his people with wisdom and grace.

Now, as the golden-red hues of twilight painted the skies, the Phoenix King stood upon a high cliff overlooking his kingdom. The Eternal Flame, the source of his power and the symbol of his rule, burned brightly within his heart. It had guided him through every challenge, every battle, and every sacrifice, lighting the way forward even in the darkest of times.

The wind, warm and gentle, whispered through the leaves of the ancient trees that lined the cliffside. It carried with it the scent of blooming flowers and fresh earth, a reminder of the life that flourished in the kingdom below. The Phoenix King closed his eyes, allowing himself a moment of quiet reflection. His journey had been long and arduous, but it had also been filled with profound lessons—lessons that had shaped him into the ruler he was today.

As he stood there, the memories of his journey began to unfold in his mind, like the pages of a book being turned one by one. He thought back to the day of his birth, when he had first emerged from the Sacred Flame as a unique phoenix with golden-red feathers, a symbol of his royal lineage. From that moment, his destiny had been intertwined with the Eternal Flame, a destiny that would lead him to face challenges that few could imagine.

He remembered the early days of his reign, when he had first learned the ways of fire and the responsibilities that came with his power. His mentor, an ancient and wise phoenix, had taught him the ancient laws of fire and resurrection, guiding him with patience and care. Those lessons had been the foundation upon which his rule was built, lessons that had taught him the importance of balance and the role of fire in the cycle of life and death.

But it was not just the teachings of his mentor that had shaped him; it was the trials he had faced, the sacrifices he had made, and the battles he had fought. The Trial of Ashes, where he had faced visions of past Phoenix Kings and learned the importance of sacrifice, had been a defining moment in his journey. It had shown him that true leadership required not just strength, but also humility and a willingness to put the needs of others before his own.

As the memories continued to flow, the Phoenix King thought of the companions who had stood by his side throughout his journey. The fire giants, with their immense strength and unwavering loyalty, had been his allies in the battles against the forces of darkness. The fire dragons, with their ancient wisdom and mastery of the elemental forces, had guided him through the most challenging of times. And then there was Ignis, the loyal ember sprite who had sacrificed himself to restore the balance, a sacrifice that had taught the Phoenix King the true cost of power.

The battles against the ancient evil and the dark phoenix had tested the Phoenix King in ways that he could never have anticipated. Those battles had been more than just physical confrontations; they had been battles of the soul, challenges that had forced him to confront the darkness within himself. The decision to merge with the dark phoenix, to embrace the darkness as a part of himself, had been the most difficult choice he had ever made. But it had also been the most transformative, a choice that had allowed him to achieve a level of balance and understanding that few could ever hope to attain.

And now, as he stood on the precipice of his reign, the Phoenix King knew that his journey was nearing its end. The lessons he had learned, the sacrifices he had made, and the wisdom he had gained—all of these had prepared him for this moment, the moment when he would pass on the Eternal Flame to the next generation, ensuring that the legacy of the Immortal Fire would continue.

The Eternal Cycle of Rebirth

The Phoenix Kingdom had always been a place of renewal, a place where the cycle of life and death was acknowledged and respected. The Eternal Flame, which burned at the heart of the kingdom, was the embodiment of that cycle—a flame that never extinguished, a flame that represented both the beginning and the end of all things.

The Phoenix King had come to understand that his role as a ruler was not just to protect the kingdom, but to ensure that the cycle of rebirth continued. He had seen the consequences of imbalance, the devastation that could be wrought when the forces of creation and destruction were not in harmony. The battles he had fought, the sacrifices he had made, were all in service of maintaining that balance, of ensuring that the cycle remained unbroken.

The Phoenix King's transformation, his merger with the dark phoenix, had been a crucial part of that understanding. It had shown him that both light and dark, creation and destruction, were essential to the cycle of rebirth. To deny one aspect was to disrupt the balance, to create a world where life could not flourish. By embracing both sides of his nature, the Phoenix King had become a guardian of the balance, a force for good in a world that was constantly changing.

But the Phoenix King also knew that his time as the guardian of the balance was coming to an end. The cycle of rebirth applied to all things, even to those who wielded the power of the Eternal Flame. Just as the phoenix was reborn from its ashes, so too must the Phoenix King pass on his legacy, ensuring that the cycle continued for generations to come.

With this in mind, the Phoenix King descended from the cliff and made his way to the Sacred Flame, the source of the Eternal Flame that burned within him. The Sacred Flame was a place of great power, a place where the forces of creation and destruction converged in perfect harmony. It was here that the Phoenix King had been born, and it was here that he would pass on the Eternal Flame to the next generation.

The journey to the Sacred Flame was a solemn one, filled with a sense of finality and purpose. The Phoenix King walked through the lush forests and vibrant fields of his kingdom, the land he had protected and nurtured for so many years. The people he encountered along the way greeted him with reverence and respect, their expressions reflecting the deep gratitude they felt for all that he had done.

As the Phoenix King approached the Sacred Flame, he was joined by the Council of the Flames, who had been his trusted advisors and allies throughout his reign. The fire giants, the fire dragons, the scholars, and the elders—all of them had played a crucial role in maintaining the balance, and all of them understood the significance of the moment that was about to unfold.

The Sacred Flame burned brightly at the center of a vast, open clearing, its radiant light illuminating the surrounding landscape. The air was filled with the scent of burning incense and the sound of crackling fire, a reminder of the power that resided within the flame. The Phoenix King approached the Sacred Flame, his heart filled with a sense of peace and fulfillment.

"My friends," the Phoenix King said, his voice calm and steady, "we have come to the end of a journey that has been filled with challenges, sacrifices, and profound lessons. The balance of our world has been restored, and the cycle of life and death, creation and destruction, continues as it should. But the time has come for me to pass on the Eternal Flame to the next generation, ensuring that the legacy of the Immortal Fire continues."

The fire giant leader, whose strength and loyalty had been unwavering, nodded solemnly. "Phoenix King, you have been a beacon of hope and renewal for our kingdom. Your wisdom and courage have guided us through the darkest of times, and we are forever grateful for all that you have done. But we understand that the cycle must continue, that the flame must be passed on."

The elder fire dragon, whose ancient wisdom had been a guiding light for the council, spoke next, his voice filled with reverence. "Phoenix King, the legacy of the Immortal Fire is one of balance, renewal, and the eternal cycle of rebirth. You have embodied these principles in every aspect of your rule, and your decision to pass on the flame is a testament to your understanding of the greater forces that govern our world."

The Phoenix King nodded, his heart filled with gratitude for the support and understanding of his council. He knew that the decision to pass on the flame was the right one, a decision that would ensure the continued prosperity and balance of the Phoenix Kingdom.

With a deep breath, the Phoenix King raised the Staff of Renewal, its light glowing with the combined energies of creation and destruction. He channeled the power of the Eternal Flame into the staff, its radiant light growing brighter and brighter until it filled the entire clearing with a brilliant, blinding light.

As the light of the Eternal Flame reached its peak, the Phoenix King closed his eyes and focused his thoughts on the cycle of rebirth, the eternal cycle that governed all things. He could feel the energy of the flame coursing through him, a powerful force that had been both his ally and his responsibility throughout his reign.

And then, with a single, decisive motion, the Phoenix King transferred the energy of the Eternal Flame into the Sacred Flame, passing on his power and his legacy to the next generation.

The Next Generation

The transfer of the Eternal Flame was a moment of profound significance, a moment that would be remembered for generations to come. The light of the Sacred Flame burned brighter than ever before, its radiant energy filling the clearing with a sense of renewal and rebirth. The Phoenix King, now without the power of the Eternal Flame, felt a sense of peace and fulfillment, knowing that the cycle would continue.

As the light of the Sacred Flame began to fade, a new figure emerged from its radiant glow—a young phoenix, born from the ashes of the Phoenix King's power. This new phoenix, with feathers of gold and crimson, was the embodiment of the next generation, the guardian of the balance who would continue the legacy of the Immortal Fire.

The young phoenix, its eyes filled with the wisdom of the ages, approached the Phoenix King, who now stood as a mentor and guide rather than a ruler. The Phoenix King looked into the eyes of the young phoenix and saw the future—a future of balance, renewal, and the eternal cycle of rebirth.

"My time as the Phoenix King has come to an end," the Phoenix King said, his voice filled with pride and contentment. "But the legacy of the Immortal Fire will continue through you. You are the guardian of the balance now, the protector of our kingdom and the keeper of the Eternal Flame. I have every confidence that you will lead with wisdom, courage, and compassion, just as I have tried to do."

The young phoenix nodded, its gaze filled with determination and resolve. "I will honor your legacy," it said, its voice filled with the energy of the Eternal Flame. "I will protect the balance and ensure that the cycle of rebirth continues. I will lead our kingdom with the same wisdom and strength that you have shown."

The Phoenix King smiled, his heart filled with a sense of fulfillment. He knew that the future of the Phoenix Kingdom was in good hands, that the next generation would continue to uphold the principles of balance and renewal that had guided his own reign.

The Council of the Flames, who had witnessed the transfer of the Eternal Flame, bowed respectfully to both the Phoenix King and the young phoenix. They understood that the cycle of leadership, like the cycle of life and death, was an essential part of the balance, and they were ready to support the new guardian of the Immortal Fire.

The Phoenix King, now free from the responsibilities of rule, felt a sense of lightness and freedom. His journey had been long and filled with challenges, but it had also been filled with profound lessons and deep understanding. He had faced his darkest fears, made difficult choices, and emerged stronger, wiser, and more complete. And now, as he prepared to step aside and allow the next generation to take the lead, he knew that his legacy would endure.

The Immortal Fire: A Legacy of Balance and Renewal

The Immortal Fire, the source of the Phoenix Kingdom's power and prosperity, was more than just a symbol of creation and destruction—it was a reminder of the eternal cycle of rebirth that governed all things. The Phoenix King had come to understand that his role as a ruler was not just to wield the power of the flame, but to ensure that the balance was maintained, that the cycle continued unbroken.

The lessons he had learned throughout his journey had been hard-won, but they had also been invaluable. He had learned the importance of balance, the need to embrace both light and dark, creation and destruction, in order to maintain harmony. He had learned the value of sacrifice, the understanding that true leadership required humility and a willingness to put the needs of others before his own. And he had learned the significance of the eternal cycle of rebirth, the knowledge that all things must eventually come to an end in order for new beginnings to emerge.

As the Phoenix King prepared to leave the Sacred Flame, he looked out over the kingdom that he had protected and nurtured for so many years. The land was vibrant and thriving, the people were at peace, and the balance was intact. The cycle of life and death, creation and destruction, continued as it always had, guided by the Eternal Flame that now burned within the young phoenix.

The Phoenix King knew that his journey had come full circle, that he had fulfilled his role as the guardian of the balance. But he also knew that the legacy of the Immortal Fire would continue, carried forward by the next generation and the generations to come. The cycle of rebirth was eternal, and with it, the principles of balance, renewal, and harmony would endure.

As the sun began to set, casting a warm, golden light over the kingdom, the Phoenix King turned to the young phoenix, his successor. "Remember the lessons you have learned," he said, his voice filled with the wisdom of his years. "Embrace the balance, honor the cycle of rebirth, and lead with compassion and understanding. The future of our kingdom rests in your hands, and I have every confidence that you will rise to the challenge."

The young phoenix nodded, its eyes filled with determination. "I will, Phoenix King. I will carry forward the legacy of the Immortal Fire and ensure that our kingdom continues to thrive. Thank you for your guidance and wisdom. I will not forget the lessons you have taught me."

With those words, the Phoenix King took one last look at the Sacred Flame, the source of his power and the symbol of his legacy. He felt a deep sense of peace, knowing that the cycle would continue, that the balance would be maintained, and that the future of the Phoenix Kingdom was secure.

And so, the Phoenix King's story came to a close, a story of light and dark, creation and destruction, and the eternal cycle of rebirth. A story that would be told and retold for generations, a story that would inspire future guardians of the balance to rise and lead with wisdom and strength.

The legacy of the Immortal Fire, the legacy of the Phoenix King, would endure—an enduring flame that would light the way for all who sought to protect the balance and ensure the continued prosperity of the world of Eldoria.

As the Phoenix King walked away from the Sacred Flame, his heart filled with the knowledge that his journey had been one of great significance, he knew that his story was not just his own, but a part of the eternal cycle that governed all things. The Immortal Fire would burn on, a symbol of hope, renewal, and the power of unity.

And as the last rays of the sun dipped below the horizon, the Phoenix King disappeared into the twilight, leaving behind a legacy that would never be forgotten—a legacy of balance, sacrifice, and the eternal cycle of rebirth.

Epilogue: The Eternal Legacy

The Birth of a Legend

The story of the Phoenix King and the Immortal Fire became more than just history; it became a legend, woven into the very fabric of the Phoenix Kingdom and passed down through the ages. The tale of his rise, his battles, his sacrifices, and ultimately, his transformation into a guardian of balance resonated deeply with those who heard it. It was a story that transcended time, a narrative that spoke to the core of what it meant to live in harmony with the forces of the world.

Generations came and went, each adding their own chapters to the legend. The Phoenix King, once a living ruler, became a symbol—a figure who embodied the principles of balance, sacrifice, and renewal. His journey, from his birth in the Sacred Flame to his final act of passing on the Eternal Flame, was recounted in songs, poems, and stories, each version carrying the essence of his wisdom and the lessons he had imparted.

In the Phoenix Kingdom, the legend of the Phoenix King was taught to every child from the moment they could understand words. Parents would tell their children of the great battles he had fought, of the sacrifices he had made, and of the ultimate choice he had faced when confronted with the dark phoenix. The story was not just a tale of heroism; it was a guide for living, a reminder that true strength came from understanding and embracing all aspects of oneself, both light and dark.

As the legend grew, it began to spread beyond the borders of the Phoenix Kingdom. Travelers and traders who visited the kingdom would hear the story and carry it with them to distant lands. In time, the tale of the Phoenix King and the Immortal Fire became known throughout Eldoria, a beacon of hope and resilience for all who heard it. It was said that the Phoenix King's wisdom had the power to change lives, to inspire those who were lost to seek balance and embrace the eternal cycle of life, death, and renewal.

The legend also became a source of strength for those who faced their own trials and challenges. In times of darkness and uncertainty, people would turn to the story of the Phoenix King, drawing inspiration from his journey and finding the courage to confront their own fears. The tale of his transformation, of his choice to embrace both light and dark, became a powerful metaphor for the struggles that all beings faced in their quest for harmony and balance.

In the centuries that followed, the legend of the Phoenix King took on a life of its own. It became more than just a story—it became a cultural touchstone, a foundation upon which the values of the Phoenix Kingdom were built. The teachings of the Phoenix King were incorporated into the kingdom's laws, its customs, and its way of life. The cycle of life and death, creation and destruction, was honored and respected, and the balance that the Phoenix King had fought so hard to maintain was preserved.

The Phoenix Kingdom in a New Era

Under the guidance of the new Phoenix King—the young phoenix who had inherited the Eternal Flame—the Phoenix Kingdom continued to thrive. The wisdom and teachings of the original Phoenix King were carried forward, ensuring that the principles of balance and renewal remained at the heart of the kingdom's governance.

The new Phoenix King, now fully grown and experienced, ruled with a deep understanding of the lessons passed down by his predecessor. He knew that the balance of the world was a delicate thing, one that required constant vigilance and care. He also understood that his role was not just to wield power, but to guide and protect his people, to ensure that the cycle of life and death continued in harmony.

The Council of the Flames, which had been a vital part of the original Phoenix King's reign, continued to serve as advisors to the new ruler. The fire giants, with their immense strength and unwavering loyalty, remained steadfast allies, helping to maintain the kingdom's infrastructure and protect its borders. The fire dragons, with their ancient wisdom and mastery of the elemental forces, continued to offer their counsel on matters of strategy and governance. The scholars, whose knowledge of the ancient texts had been invaluable, remained dedicated to preserving and expanding the understanding of the balance and the Eternal Flame.

The Phoenix Kingdom, now in a new era of peace and prosperity, became a model for other realms. The principles of balance, renewal, and the eternal cycle of rebirth were not just taught within the kingdom; they were shared with the world. Diplomats and emissaries from other lands came to the Phoenix Kingdom to learn from its leaders, to study the teachings of the Phoenix King, and to bring those lessons back to their own people.

The schools and academies that had been established during the original Phoenix King's reign flourished, becoming centers of learning and innovation. Students from all over Eldoria traveled to the Phoenix Kingdom to study the ways of balance and to learn the secrets of the Immortal Fire. These institutions produced scholars, philosophers, and leaders who carried the teachings of the Phoenix King into the wider world, spreading his legacy far beyond the borders of the kingdom.

In time, the Phoenix Kingdom became known as the "Land of the Immortal Flame," a place where the forces of creation and destruction were in perfect harmony, where the cycle of life and death was honored and respected. The kingdom's prosperity was a testament to the power of balance, a living example of what could be achieved when the lessons of the Phoenix King were embraced.

The people of the Phoenix Kingdom lived in harmony with the land and with each other, guided by the principles of balance and renewal. They understood that their prosperity was not a given, but something that had to be nurtured and protected. They honored the memory of the original Phoenix King, not just through stories and songs, but through their actions—by living lives that were in harmony with the world around them.

The Eternal Flame as a Symbol of Hope

The Eternal Flame, which had once been the source of the Phoenix King's power, became a symbol of hope and resilience for all who beheld it. It was said that the flame contained the essence of the Phoenix King's wisdom, that its light could guide those who were lost and bring peace to those who were troubled. Pilgrims from distant lands would journey to the Sacred Flame, seeking its blessings and hoping to find answers to the questions that weighed upon their hearts.

The flame, burning brightly in the heart of the Phoenix Kingdom, was a reminder of the eternal cycle of rebirth—a cycle that had been upheld and protected by the Phoenix King. It was a symbol of the resilience of the kingdom, of its ability to overcome challenges and emerge stronger, wiser, and more united. The flame's light, which had guided the Phoenix King through his trials, now served as a beacon for all who sought to live in harmony with the world.

In the years that followed, the Eternal Flame became the center of many important rituals and ceremonies. It was customary for new leaders, not just within the Phoenix Kingdom but also from other realms, to visit the flame before assuming their roles. They would stand before the Sacred Flame, reflecting on the lessons of the Phoenix King and seeking the wisdom needed to guide their people.

The flame also became a source of comfort for those who were grieving or facing difficult times. The people believed that the flame could bring peace to troubled souls, that its light could dispel the darkness of despair and bring hope to those who had lost their way. Families who had suffered loss would gather at the Sacred Flame, finding solace in its warmth and strength in its enduring presence.

The story of the Phoenix King, passed down through the ages, was a constant reminder of the power of resilience and the importance of balance. It was a story that spoke to the heart of what it meant to be human, to face challenges and overcome them, to embrace all aspects of oneself—both light and dark—in order to live a life of harmony and purpose.

As the legend of the Phoenix King continued to inspire future generations, the Eternal Flame became more than just a symbol of his legacy; it became a symbol of the potential that lay within all beings—the potential to rise from the ashes, to find balance within oneself, and to contribute to the greater good of the world.

The Legacy Lives On

The legacy of the Phoenix King lived on through the actions of those who followed in his footsteps. The new Phoenix King, who had inherited the Eternal Flame, ruled with the same wisdom and compassion that had guided his predecessor. He understood that his role was not just to maintain the balance, but to ensure that the lessons of the Phoenix King were passed on to future generations.

The Council of the Flames, who had served the original Phoenix King with loyalty and dedication, continued to play a crucial role in the governance of the kingdom. They understood that the balance was a delicate thing, one that required constant vigilance and care. They also understood that the legacy of the Phoenix King was not just about power or rule; it was about wisdom, compassion, and the understanding that true strength came from the integration of all aspects of oneself.

The people of the Phoenix Kingdom, who had lived through the trials and challenges of the past, now looked to the future with hope and optimism. They knew that their kingdom was a place of balance and harmony, a place where the cycle of life and death, creation and destruction, was honored and respected. They also knew that the legacy of the Phoenix King was something that they carried within themselves—a legacy that would guide them in their own lives and in the lives of those who would come after them.

The story of the Phoenix King, which had once been a tale of heroism and sacrifice, became a story of hope and renewal. It was a story that reminded people that no matter how dark the times might seem, there was always a way forward, always a path to balance and harmony. The Phoenix King's journey, from his birth in the Sacred Flame to his final act of passing on the Eternal Flame, was a testament to the power of resilience, the importance of balance, and the eternal cycle of rebirth.

As the years passed, the legend of the Phoenix King became a part of the collective memory of the people of Eldoria. It was a story that was told and retold, a story that was celebrated in festivals and honored in rituals. The Phoenix King's name became synonymous with wisdom and strength, and his legacy became a guiding light for all who sought to live in harmony with the world.

The Eternal Flame, which had once been the source of the Phoenix King's power, continued to burn brightly in the heart of the kingdom. It was a reminder that the cycle of life and death, creation and destruction, was eternal, and that the balance that the Phoenix King had fought so hard to maintain would endure for generations to come.

A New Beginning

The story of the Phoenix King, though now a legend, was not the end—it was the beginning of a new chapter in the history of the Phoenix Kingdom and the world of Eldoria. The lessons learned, the sacrifices made, and the balance restored were not just events of the past; they were the foundation upon which the future would be built.

The new Phoenix King, who had inherited the Eternal Flame, understood this truth. He knew that his role was not just to rule, but to guide and protect, to ensure that the balance was maintained and that the legacy of the Phoenix King continued. He also knew that he was part of a greater cycle, a cycle that had been upheld by those who came before him and that would continue with those who would come after him.

As he stood before the Sacred Flame, the new Phoenix King reflected on the journey that had brought him to this moment. He thought of the original Phoenix King, whose wisdom and courage had set the stage for the prosperity and harmony that now graced the kingdom. He thought of the challenges that had been faced and overcome, and of the lessons that had been learned along the way.

He also thought of the future, of the generations who would come after him, and of the role he would play in shaping that future. He knew that his reign would be one of balance and renewal, a reign that would honor the legacy of the Phoenix King and ensure that the cycle of life and death, creation and destruction, continued unbroken.

As the new Phoenix King looked out over his kingdom, he felt a deep sense of responsibility but also a sense of purpose. He knew that the legacy of the Phoenix King was not just a story to be told, but a living truth to be lived. He knew that the Eternal Flame, which burned brightly within him, was a symbol of hope and resilience, a beacon that would guide him and his people through whatever challenges lay ahead.

And so, with the lessons of the Phoenix King as his guide, the new Phoenix King began his reign—a reign that would be marked by balance, harmony, and the eternal cycle of rebirth. The story of the Phoenix King, now a legend passed down through the ages, would continue to inspire and guide all who sought to live in harmony with the world.

The Eternal Flame, the symbol of the Phoenix King's legacy, would continue to burn brightly, a reminder that the cycle of life and death, creation and destruction, was eternal, and that the balance would endure.

The story of the Phoenix King was a story of light and dark, creation and destruction, and the eternal cycle of rebirth. It was a story that had shaped the past, defined the present, and would guide the future—a story that would live on in the hearts and minds of the people of Eldoria for generations to come.

And as the new Phoenix King looked out over his kingdom, the flames of the Eternal Flame burning brightly in the distance, he knew that the legacy of the Immortal Fire would continue—a legacy of balance, resilience, and the eternal cycle of life, death, and renewal.

The legend of the Phoenix King would never fade, for it was a story of the human spirit, a story of hope and renewal, a story that would inspire future generations to seek balance, to embrace the cycle of life, death, and rebirth, and to live lives of harmony and purpose.

The story of the Phoenix King, though now a legend, would never be forgotten, for it was a story that was eternal, a story that would continue to guide and inspire all who sought the light of the Eternal Flame.

Don't miss out!

Visit the website below and you can sign up to receive emails whenever Patrick William Lee publishes a new book. There's no charge and no obligation.

https://books2read.com/r/B-A-FLRYB-WJGTE

BOOKS2READ

Connecting independent readers to independent writers.

Did you love *The Phoenix King*? Then you should read *The Mermaid's Whisper*[1] by Patrick William Lee!

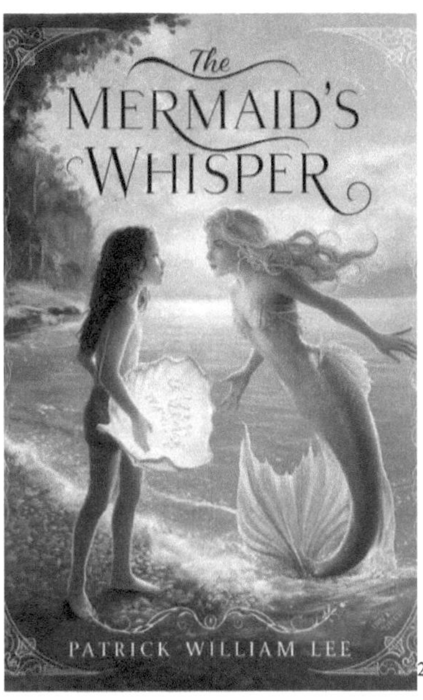

In the coastal village of Marinia, young Elara discovers an enchanted shell that leads her to Seraphina, a cursed mermaid. Together, they embark on a perilous quest to break the curse, battling mythical creatures and confronting dark forces. As Elara rises as the guardian of the shore, her legacy endures, inspiring future generations to protect the ocean. "The Mermaid's Whisper" is a captivating tale of bravery, friendship, and the timeless bond between humans and the sea.

---

1. https://books2read.com/u/3kwEDN

2. https://books2read.com/u/3kwEDN

About the Author

Patrick William Lee is a renowned author celebrated for his enchanting tales of magic and wonder. Specializing in the genres of fairy tales, folk tales, legends, and mythology, Patrick weaves stories that transport readers to fantastical realms where the impossible becomes reality. With a deep love for folklore and a talent for crafting timeless narratives, his books captivate the imaginations of readers young and old. When he's not writing, Patrick enjoys exploring ancient forests, studying mythical creatures, and sharing his passion for storytelling with audiences around the world. His works continue to inspire and delight, leaving a lasting impact on the world of literature.